Metaphorosis

July 2022

Beautifully made speculative fiction

Also from Metaphorosis

<u>Metaphorosis Magazine</u>

Metaphorosis: Best of 20xx
Metaphorosis 20xx: The Complete Stories
annual issues, from 2016

Monthly issues

<u>Plant Based Press</u>

Best Vegan Science Fiction & Fantasy
annual issues, 2016-2020

from B. Morris Allen:
Chambers of the Heart: speculative stories
Susurrus
Allenthology: Volume I
Tocsin: and other stories
Start with Stones: collected stories
Metaphorosis: a collection of stories

<u>Verdage</u>

Reading 5X5 x3: Changes
Reading 5X5 x2: Duets
Score – an SFF symphony
Reading 5X5: Readers' Edition
Reading 5X5: Writers' Edition

<u>Vestige</u>

The Nocturnals, by Mariah Montoya

Metaphorosis

July 2022

---

edited by
B. Morris Allen

ISSN: 2573-136X (online)
ISBN: 978-1-64076-232-9 (e-book)
ISBN: 978-1-64076-233-6 (paperback)

Metaphorosis
a magazine of speculative fiction
from
Metaphorosis Publishing

Neskowin

July 2022

The Eye of the Goddess

Samuel Parr

The Sololfursson had said Ingolfur was too weak to reach the Goddess's Isle. Their laughter haunted him for three days across the sea, yet finally he found the island's skirt of silver mist, as the druids had promised. The vapour shelled him in silver, softening the itch of his bloodstained skin and deepening his certainty. This place had been his destiny since he was born.

Yet when the mist lifted, he felt a flicker of doubt. The twilight sun revealed only a spit of summer forest, girdled by basalt cliffs; after twenty years of stories, he had expected the Isle to fill the sky.

Still, he kept on rowing. The Goddess *must* be here. It was only fitting that, like him, the Isle hid its true nature. As he entered a small cove armoured in shingle, he imagined the land itself reaching out to greet him. For a moment, the fear he had carried across the long waves disappeared.

Then he saw the man, waiting still as granite on the shore.

He looked a common shepherd — a cloak of rough wool, eyes of dull flint, and skin carved by too many winters — but Ingolfur felt a spike of dread. The druids' adage echoed in his ear: "No man who seeks the Isle stays." This place should be home only to beasts and birds.

Yet wasn't Ingolfur a great warrior, still cloaked in the blood and ash of his last battle? He groped for the comfort of his sword hilt; this shepherd was the one who should fear.

"Hail, saltwalker," he called as Ingolfur beached, his voice cracked but strong. "I've goat's milk and fruit wine, and would be pleased to share." He spread his hands. "My hall is draughty, but plenty wide for two."

"Do you follow the Cross or the Moon?" Ingolfur asked, proud of how fearlessly his voice barrelled through the salt wind. The challenge made him sound a true Sololfursson.

The man laughed. "The Moon, lad, and her Goddess, fool as I'd be to say otherwise to one of Sololfur's swords."

"You know my order?"

"Aye. Though you're young to have taken the vows."

"I am old enough," Ingolfur snapped. "And it is my vows that have led me here. This is the Isle of Dragons?"

"Some call it that," the man said, eyes narrowing. "Others ask for the Moon's Rest, or the Soul's Mirror. But aye, lad. The Goddess is here."

Ingolfur kept his face cold, but excitement bloomed inside him.

"I am Afi Haraldsson," the old man continued. "What may I call—"

"I am Ingolfur of the Sons," Ingolfur interrupted. "I seek the Goddess's judgement. I have lamellar and mail, a blade of pure starsteel, and the silver crosses of seven knights. Guide me to her, and all of it is yours."

"Seven knights?" Afi grinned, and Ingolfur's fist curled. This hermit doubted him, like all the others. "Aye, I'll guide you, though you're an unusual Son, lad."

He tapped the ship's prow with his foot. "In my day, Sololfur's warriors would never travel alone, or in such a ship."

Ingolfur flinched. Afi had noticed the long-bodied carvings wriggling over every inch of the ship, each flickering a forked tongue. The other Sons had gouged them there after they chained him; a suitable shape, they claimed, for a coward.

Yet he would prove them wrong. He unsheathed his sword, reaching for the clarity he had felt when he spoke the vows of the Sololfursson, two years ago.

I swear my soul to protecting the people of the Moon.

The boat split in two with a single blow. The planks danced across the pebbles, to be lapped by the waves.

Afi's gentle smile did not waver.

"That was unwise," he said.

"It was not." Ingolfur looked to the sky; above, a herring gull soared, the setting sunlight casting it into a sliver of gold. "When I leave this island, it will be on wings."

Afi led him up a steep cliffside path, littered with the skeletons of shearwater chicks. When they crested the top, heathland rolled out for a few hundred feet before the forest engulfed it. The air was thick with the scents of heather pollen and rotting seaweed. Apart from the single gull, the sky was empty. After seeing the endless temples of the Cross Lands, Ingolfur was disappointed that this, the greatest of his people's myths, was so mundane.

"Beautiful, isn't she?" Afi said. "Used to be folk of all creeds came here, but you're the first for many a season."

"You have been on this Isle a long time?" Ingolfur said. "Were you here to guide Sololfur too?"

Afi's mouth twitched. "Afraid not, lad. Never guided the dragon lord."

Ingolfur felt a sting of disappointment. The story of Sololfur was woven as deep within him as the Isle's. Two decades ago, the great clan father had left his people as a man, and sought the Eye of the Goddess. He had never returned, but his transformation had been depicted in crafted steel in the Sololfursson's Hall: not as bird or beast, but as a winged dragon, the ultimate symbol of warriorhood. The druids sang that he had flown on to the Cross homeland, to fight the Knights there. Ingolfur had stared at the carved beast for long hours in his childhood, feeling the longing in his gut. If only he had had a dragon's strength, he wouldn't have grown up alone.

Afi peered upwards. "There's someone just as impressive for you to meet, though," he said. "You'll need her approval, if I'm to guide you."

The herring gull was coming closer, transforming from a fragment of light into a snow-feathered bird, its beak a golden spear-tip dipped in blood. Afi grinned as it landed on his shoulder.

"This is Kari," he said gently. "She wanted to see if you would gut me before she said hello."

The herring gull cocked an eye of speckled brown at Ingolfur, blinking once before giving a keening cry.

"Ah, she likes you!" Afi said, caressing her neck. "Are the skies clear, my light?" She bobbed. Ingolfur's throat tightened.

"She has received the Goddess's gifts?" he said.

Afi nodded.

Wonder filled him. The white of the gull's feathers reminded him of the druid's cave paintings on the mainland: ancient images daubed in charcoal and crushed shell, showing a woman in a black pool, before a white orb inscribed with an eye — the Moon of the Goddess, Lady of Seasons and Tides and all true change. Its light rippled down, casting the woman's reflection into the water: not that of a human, but of a white seal. In the next painting, the woman was gone, and only the seal remained, swimming away into an ocean of shadow.

"It's true, then," he said. "You stand before the Goddess's Eye, and she reflects your soul's shape?"

"A druid tell you that?" Afi said, eyes glinting. "Aye, lad. You're right enough."

Ingolfur shivered. He had a sudden urge to reach out and touch the bird's feathers, but he fought it back. That was not how a Sololfursson acted.

"I admire seekers such as you," Afi said. "It's an act of great bravery, to hunt such truth."

"Truth? I know my soul, old man. It is a dragon's, like Sololfur's before me." He hated how amusement danced in the old man's eyes. "You doubt me?"

"Nay, lad, only curious. What makes you so sure?"

"My soul echoes his." Ingolfur's voice thickened with pride. "Always, he has inspired me. On the mainland, he had everything; the oaths of a hundred warriors, a mighty hall of golden oak, and two young sons to carry his legacy. Yet he left them behind to come here. He gave *everything*, to protect his people. I too am willing to make such a sacrifice."

"A mighty calling, for one so young," Afi murmured. But he wasn't even listening, staring past Ingolfur to the ocean. "And it seems you're merely the first wonder today, Ingolfur Dragon-Soul, to arrive on the Goddess's shore."

The sea was darkening, but the mist still shone. In its depths, a silhouette loomed.

A sailing boat.

A sinuous shape writhed inside Ingolfur's gut.

They had followed him here.

"Likely a lost fisher," Afi said, stroking Kari. "If so, they know not to beach."

Yet Ingolfur was already moving. The clotted shadow of the forest beckoned him, to melt into it, and become something scaled and slithering amongst the undergrowth.

Before the trees, he braved a look back. The shadow had disappeared. Nothing approached the island.

But how many other ships might be out there, hiding just behind the innocent face of the mists?

"Looked like you were fleeing, lad," Afi said as he entered the trees.

Ingolfur managed a laugh. "A Sololfursson does not spook at a fishing boat, old man."

Afi chuckled as he led them amongst twilit maples and pines, navigating a floor of brambles heavy with dewberries. Kari flitted ghost-like from tree to tree. Something crunched underneath Ingolfur's feet; tiny bones. They stank of rancid meat.

The night had nearly closed in when Afi stopped by a grey-barked oak at the edge of a stream. He retrieved a pile of dry sticks from a hollow under the tree's roots, then pulled out a sparking flint.

"We continue," Ingolfur said.

The flash of the flint lit Afi's frown. "We don't, lad," he said. "No matter how much you brandish that starsteel. I'd prefer dealing with an angry Son to seeking the Eye at night." He pulled out a skin from his waist. "But if you promise not to slay me, I'll share my wine."

Ingolfur hesitated, hearing the Sons' laughter in his ear. A Sololfursson did not obey the commands of hermits; he should make Afi continue, at sword's point if he had to.

But surely a Son could also be magnanimous? And his armour felt heavy...

He sat. Afi whooped and handed him the skin. Ingolfur took a sip, then cursed.

"Tastes of fire and piss," he hissed.

"Ferment it myself," Afi said. "Vintage of the Goddess. Drink, lad — there's nought else I can offer you but nuts and berries."

"You have no meat?"

"No, lad. Never hunt on the Isle."

The alcohol was strong, at least, and it helped soften the ship's silhouette in Ingolfur's mind. This was a far cry from the Sons' camps. There, every Son sparred for the right to eat, with any deemed wanting going hungry while forced to serve the rest. Yet here, the forest was quiet; no bird song, no scampering of beasts, only the stream's murmur and the fire's crackle. Ingolfur felt his breathing slow.

Something shifted in the darkness. He started, hand on his hilt.

A mountain hare emerged to sit at the fire's edge, the red light glittering off eyes of aquamarine. A green-eyed fox soon joined it, sitting next to its prey to stare at Ingolfur. His skin prickled.

"Bear them no mind," Afi said. "They only like the flames. I think they remember them."

The beasts sat there for a long time as the night deepened. Their gazes were gentle, but they irked Ingolfur. He felt like they were an audience, judging his worth.

"Remove your armour, lad," Afi said. "It must weigh you down."

"A Son doesn't remove his plate until the battle is done."

"Oh? I've been wondering about that. Where *are* the brothers of your order? In my time, whether they camped, sailed, or raided, the Sololfursson did so together."

Ingolfur flinched. The fire's crackle was suddenly like laughter. "I was named dragon-souled," he said. "And so only I am worthy to follow Sololfur's footsteps. I was a warrior of great might on the mainland. The youngest Son to ever be taken on a salt ranging into the Cross lands."

"Aye? Must have been a sight."

"It was," Ingolfur said, voice warming. "We sailed into their lands for five days to reach their monastery, and their god. You should have seen it; a mountain's worth of stone in a single building, more treasure than a hundred dowries, and windows of hard light. Yet none of it could stop us paying them back for what they did."

"And what had they done?" Afi said.

"What they have done for generations. Steal our flocks. Steal our land. Steal our children." He found he was spitting the words. "They took my brother, when I was a boy."

"Ah. I'm sorry, lad."

Ingolfur shook his head, remembering the pure-white sails of the Knights on the horizon. He and Talolfur had been building a raft on the beach, so that they could seek the Isle. His brother had told Ingolfur to fetch the Sons, but he had been too scared, and instead hid in the grass. His insides curled in shame at the memory.

"I was weak then," he said. "I could not stop it. But the Sololfursson trained me to be strong. We came upon that monastery like dragons, and the Cross fled like snakes." His hand twitched at the memory of his blade, cleaving through the back of his seventh knight. "The priests barricaded themselves in their church without even facing us, yet we were the Sons of Sololfur Dragon-Soul, and would not be denied." He remembered the laughter of the men as they had stacked the pitch-tarred wood against the doors. How their war chief laughed louder than all of them, and ordered Ingolfur to set it alight.

Afi frowned, lifting a hand. "Hold a moment," he murmured. "When I was on the mainland, the Cross would have boys in their churches, to sing their God's praises. You mention the priests, and the knights, but what of them?"

Ingolfur's hand twitched again. "I saw none such," he said. "We are not child-killers, old man. That is why I am here, after all. When I take the dragon shape, the Cross will take no more children. I will fly high above our shores, and burn any knight that dare come close."

Afi nodded slowly. Kari gave a soft coo, as if soothing him. Ingolfur flushed; he had forgotten the beasts a moment. The fox and rabbit were watching him still.

Then he tensed.

Another eye glittered in the darkness.

Afi followed his gaze. "Another visitor?" he said softly. "You are welcome, at our fire."

Ingolfur leapt up at the creature that slithered into the light. The flame danced off its long body, revealing scales patterned into light and shadow. Its tongue tasted the air.

"A snake," he hissed.

Afi lifted his hands. "Just another friend, seeking the fire's comfort."

Ingolfur shook his head. When it stopped, the snake was near invisible amongst the leaves. The memory of his ship's wriggling carvings flashed, and he heard Sword Chief Falfur's voice in his ear, the chief's voice dark as the sea's depths.

"We defile your body, and mark you snake-souled."

"Any Son would be shamed," Ingolfur spat. "To have their soul revealed in such a shape." He drew his sword. "Make it leave. I won't suffer such a coward at *my* fire."

"Hush, lad. Don't shout, not this late-"

"Make it leave!" Ingolfur roared.

His cry split the night.

And, in the long dark beyond the fire, another scream answered.

It ravaged the air; a sound between a fox's howl, an eagle's screech, and a man's cry, but a hundred times rawer, piercing with its sudden need.

It sounded close.

The rabbit and fox bolted, while the snake slipped into the leaves. Ingolfur scanned the darkness. A beast? Beyond the fire, the night crouched everywhere, and against it his starsteel seemed an inconsequential slip of light.

A Son would stand fast. A Son would be brave.

The air suddenly reeked with carrion, and a shadow crossed the moon.

Ingolfur yelped and kicked at the fire, smothering the flames. In the darkness, he pressed himself to the earth, filled with a vast, familiar fear.

"*We name you snake-souled,*" the war chief whispered again.

Afi's voice, when it came, was calm. "Needn't have done that, lad."

"What is that?" Ingolfur hissed.

"The reason we're waiting here. Have no fear; it mislikes coming amongst the trees, and will slumber tomorrow."

Ingolfur shivered, unable to rise. "It sounded like a beast," he said. "Wounded, perhaps."

"Wounded? Aye, I suppose so. Take it as a warning; not all the Goddess's gifts are good, lad. Some men's souls are unnatural. And unnatural souls have unnatural reflections. But it will not come into the trees. Sleep. Regain your strength."

He was right, it seemed; Ingolfur waited for a long time, yet nothing disturbed the forest. Yet he couldn't sleep, not with the beast's scream echoing in his ears. Eventually he rose to pace and pace in the dark, finally falling into an uneasy drowsing far from Afi's relit fire. He dreamt of hands pushing him down, forcing his body to fold and coil in on itself, while men laughed with the roars of dragons, ecstatic in their violence.

Ingolfur woke to Afi standing over him, a sword in his hand.

He was on his feet before he realised the blade was sheathed in a scabbard of tattered leather, the hilt rotten with rust. Afi's eyes creased.

"Not for you, lad."

"You didn't have that yesterday," Ingolfur said. He would have noticed.

Even simple steel swords were a luxury few could afford.

Afi's glance flickered to a tree branch, where Kari perched, preening her feathers. "Yesterday there wasn't a longship approaching my island."

"What?" His gut writhed. "Did it have a dragon's head?"

Afi's eyes were very still. "So, you know it."

They had found him.

"They are other seekers," he said, managing to keep his face impassive, as a Son should. "We must make haste. I do not want to compete for the Goddess's attention. By the time they find the Eye, I will be soaring over the sea."

It was all he could do not to break into a run as he followed Afi through the forest. He pictured the dragonship: how the warriors would fill the fifteen benches, oars defying the waves. How they would pour from the ship in formation, swords naked. How they would laugh as they found his tracks.

Compared to them, the forest was insultingly peaceful. The sunlight shone slight and silvery, while a cool wind brought the scents of loam and rain. It would have been beautiful, if not for the silence; he listened for the voices of his pursuers, but there was not even birdsong. Yet he caught the glint of eyes watching from the trees twice, and his feet crunched on more bones tangled in the brambles. As they went, the skeletons grew more common, and larger: rabbits and squirrels, gulls and guillemots, twice a goat, and once a deer. Beasts died in any forest, yet these bones were blackened and crazed, and often scattered, as if they had been dropped from a great height. Each had been picked clean, but was still heavy with the scent of rotting meat.

It was a relief when the trees finally cleared, revealing the crash of the northern shore and clean salt air. Afi called a halt at the forest's edge, murmuring several things to Kari before the gull took wing.

"She will watch for the others?" Ingolfur said.

"Aye. Always does."

The shoreline was slow going. The tide was receding, leaving rockpools slippery with seaweed. Ingolfur glanced into one; beneath his broken reflection, hermit crabs sheltered, their shells striated with red and white, retreating into themselves under his shadow.

"How far?" he said.

Afi pointed beyond the rock pools to a beach of shingles, a mirror to the cove where Ingolfur had landed. It ended in two great flanks of rock, leading into a cave.

"At the seat of the tides, the Eye rests," he intoned. "There the Goddess will show the shape of your soul."

"I will be a dragon," Ingolfur said. His jaw tightened as Afi frowned. "You doubt —"

Kari's cry cut Ingolfur off. Afi's eyes widened.

"Run, lad!" he cried.

Ingolfur twisted, expecting to see the Sons howling from the forest.

A shadow passed overhead, trailing the stink of rot.

The creature that slammed onto the rocks came to Ingolfur in fragments. A winged body the size of an auroch, armoured in scales black as basalt. A bird's head with eyes weeping shadow. Forelegs ending in the vast hands of a man.

Then the parts resolved into a single beast. Ingolfur stepped back, gut coiling.

The creature spread fans of greasy feathers, and screamed.

Then, slicking from the great beak, came words.

"*Raid we shall, over the salt road,*" it exhaled, in a voice like a storm wind.

He ran.

Ahead, Afi sprinted to the cave. Ingolfur tried to match him, but his mail weighed him down, and he stumbled in a shallow rock pool. A shadow surrounded him, then whistled past; the beast smashed into the shore to his right, skittering pebbles.

"*Son son burn we shall.*"

Ingolfur's heart convulsed at the dreadful voice. Afi had reached the cave's mouth, but stopped in its shadow, and called something. The cave looked too small for the beast, yet the sound of crashing shingle came closer and closer as the creature gave chase. The scent of hot metal and blood and spoiled meat assaulted Ingolfur. He readied himself for the touch of those vast fingers.

Yet, just as the footsteps crescendoed, they stopped. The beast whispered, right in his ear.

"*Son my son it is good so good you are here.*"

Whimpering, Ingolfur found a final burst of speed, and slipped past Afi into the darkness.

He ran until the screams were only an echo behind him. His eyes adjusted to a tunnel lit by distant sunlight. A shadow approached, and he caught a flash of trembling white. Kari.

"I thought a Son like yourself might face such a beast," Afi said, breathing hard.

Ingolfur groaned, shaking at the old man's words. Afi was right. They had all been right. He was a snake. A coward. Unfit to be a Sololfursson.

"Calm, now," Afi said. "No shame in wisdom. If you faced Sololfur, you would have been killed."

His voice was gentle. This was not how you spoke to a Son. Ingolfur shut his eyes, longing to escape.

Then he raised his head.

"That...was Sololfur?"

"Aye, lad. Different from your legends?"

"But..." Ingolfur exhaled. That creature was nothing like the depictions of the dragon lord from his childhood.

Monster, he thought.

Yet the ground had shaken under its feet. Its skin glittered brighter than mail, and it had *flown*. How could any Cross Knight stand against such a creature?

"He has terrorised this Isle for decades," Afi said. "Yet it has been years since I have seen him in the sun. It burns him, as do the forest's leaves." He stroked Kari's still-shaking wings. "We have guided dozens to the Eye without him daring the daylight. Yet now you are here, he wakes."

"He spoke to me," Ingolfur said.

"He *spoke* to you, boy?" Was that envy in the old man's voice? "What did he say?"

It had been nonsense. A stream of sound. But then...

My son.

He had called Ingolfur his son.

Ingolfur closed his eyes, letting that truth sink into him.

Afi sighed. "It matters not, I suppose. Now you understand, lad. Seek a different shape."

But Ingolfur found he was being filled with a bright, hard certainty.

"All my life," he said, rising. "My people have called me weak. A shame, to my people, my Goddess, my father. Still, I swore to protect them." He exhaled, remembering the long years as a child staring at the sea, hoping to see a longship. "I always knew I would follow my father here."

"Father?" Afi said, stepping back.

Ingolfur laughed, suddenly elated. "Yes, old man. I am the son of Sololfur, by oath *and* blood. And out there, he *claimed* me. Take me to the Eye, Afi Haraldsson. As heir to the Dragon Jarl, I command it."

Afi's hand twitched towards his hilt. "You are his spawn?" he growled. "Then no."

Ingolfur drew his sword. Yet before he could swing, Kari darted forward, talons wrapping around his wrist. Her brown eyes gazed at him with a human gentleness, as if seeking something in him.

Then his hand was on her body. Part of him quailed – the slithering weakling, which the Sons had always mocked – but he pushed the thoughts away. This was what a Son would do.

"Lead me, Afi," he said. Kari shrieked as he tightened his fingers. He could feel the whisper of her heartbeat.

The old man's face became very cold, but he finally obeyed. He led Ingolfur through a honeycomb of sea caves, full of soft sand and the crash of the ocean. They came to a tunnel toothed with quartz, so narrow that the crystals pricked at Ingolfur's armour. It eventually widened, and Ingolfur gasped.

A vast rock pool stretched out in all directions, churning like the Far Salt Maelstrom he had once seen from the longship. Natural shafts in the ceiling let silver light dance on its tattered surface – moonlight, despite the fact it was surely still daytime. On its shores, everything was changing. Bindweed vines softened into moss as they climbed from the saltwater to the dripping stone wall. Great thickets of seaweed gleamed with fish eggs. Some hatched as he watched, their trembling bodies pulled away by the pool's flow.

"The Eye," Afi said. "I hope it's worth it, lad."

"What do I do?"

"Step into the water. The Goddess will reveal the shape of your soul. To accept it, you need only cast yourself into the waves."

"You have served me well," Ingolfur said. He released Kari, but she just fluttered to his shoulder. He growled and pushed her away, then stepped into the pool, the cold water pulling at him like a question.

"Goddess," he said. "I am Ingolfur, Son of Sololfur. Like my father before me, see my soul. Grant me the power to protect my people."

In the centre of the whirlpool was a light. It grew as he waded deeper, a flickering red and gold.

He understood. It was the light of the monastery, after the Sons had torched its timber outbuildings. He could hear their laughter, and the thin wails of those inside.

"I fought well there," he said. "I slew three knights, in your name."

The light softened, into the gold of a twilit sky.

The water was up to his neck now. It tightened around him, making him thrash to stay afloat. And there, in the fragments of the maelstrom, he saw his reflection, and the shape the Goddess offered him.

A serpent, flat on its belly, hiding in the grass.

He turned away with a cry.

Afi's sword whistled past his ear.

Ingolfur was unsure whether horror or instinct got him out of that pool, but the next thing he knew, he was gasping on the rocks, sword in hand as Afi advanced. The old man's tattered sheath hung by his side, yet he held no rusted blade, but a white-blue length of steel, tempered and folded into the brilliance of a star.

"Sorry, lad," he said. "But I won't allow another dragon."

He leapt with a viper's speed. Ingolfur barely turned his thrust, and Afi easily sidestepped his counter swipe. Only instinct saved him from the next five attacks; Afi's form was honed, his grip changing expertly as he moved from thrust to cut to guard. Yet it was more than that. He struck to kill. Like a Son. Ingolfur tried to deflect, but the serpent's shape flashed in his mind. His guard opened for a heartbeat, and Afi's sword arced into a killing blow.

A white shape flickered between them – Kari. Afi flinched, angling his blade away as Ingolfur counter-struck, sword rasping against Afi's, bringing their faces close.

"Why?" he screamed. "Why didn't I see a dragon?"

Afi's eyes widened. "It means you're not your father, lad."

"No!" Ingolfur shouted. "The bitch got it wrong!"

But, a traitorous voice whispered inside him, how much easier would it be, to hold a snake's simple form? How much safer, to slip under the cover of grass and heather, and hide from their laughter?

What had made him flinch in the pool: the snake's shape, or the fact it had pleased him?

He collapsed, sword clattering on the stone. He had failed. He bowed his head, ready for Afi's blow.

Instead, the old man knelt.

"It seems," he said. "That Kari doesn't want me to kill you."

"Do it," Ingolfur whispered. "Give me a Son's death."

Afi hesitated, before placing a hand on Ingolfur's shoulder.

"Let me tell you a tale," he murmured. "That might give you hope." He sighed, and the weariness in the sound made him seem truly old. "When Sololfur came to this isle, lad, he wasn't alone. I came with him, as his most trusted thane. We'd heard the stories of the Goddess's power, and after one hundred raids together, we believed we were heroes. But after so long killing, all we cared about was blood. And so, when we came to the Eye, the Goddess showed us what our souls had become;

not the beings of fire we thought ourselves, but monsters of rot, with tattered wings that would not carry us across the sea."

"Your father was entranced. He ordered me to take the shape with him — and I was tempted, aye. But the truth of what I was also horrified me. Your father was furious when I refused him." He gave a low laugh. "He attacked me, and I fled as he changed."

"That was when Kari found me. She brought me fish, and led me through the deeper tunnels, where I could escape Sololfur's new form. It hurt, to see her body's purity, when I knew mine was so twisted. It hurt more to feel the kindness she gave me; kindness I didn't deserve. I had brought pain and suffering to her Isle – Sololfur and I had sworn to protect our people, same as you, yet the dragon was killing all he could. And so I repeated the oath I had taken as a Sololfursson: I would protect her from him, as well as all the others seeking the Goddess."

"And so I did, lad. For two decades, I have learnt Sololfur's ways, and guided our people across this Isle. And in doing so, I have come to a revelation. Your reflection can change. Now I look in the

Eye, and witness another form." His voice cracked. "But I cannot take it. Not while Sololfur still soars."

Slowly, Ingolfur lifted his head.

"Your reflection changed?" he croaked.

Afi nodded. "What do you think the Goddess sees, through her Eye?" he whispered. "The druids claim she reflects our soul's shape, but how does she see it? After twenty years, I think I have found my answer. It's our desires, lad. Our desires, after all, are the expressions of our change. Our desires are the language of our souls. The Goddess sees them and grants us the shape to fulfil them." He stroked Ingolfur's hair, like a mother might. "So I ask you, lad, before the Goddess. What do you want to be, truly? And what's stopping you from becoming it?"

Ingolfur gritted his teeth, the silence yawning until he could bear it no longer.

"All my life, I have been afraid," he whispered. "But all my life, I wanted to be a Sololfursson. I thought if only I pretended, if I ignored my fear, I could become so. It worked for a while. But then we came to that monastery. And there *were* children. Falfur, our war chief, ordered me to lock the boys in the nave and burn the monastery down. To finally prove I was my father's son. I *wanted* to do it, but the Cross boys were crying out, and suddenly I was back on that beach, hearing Talolfur's screams.

"I couldn't set the monastery alight. I was too scared." The words came like bile. "And so, they overpowered me, and took me to the cliff face. Before the Goddess's tides, Falfur named my soul a snake's, doomed to run and hide forever. Yet I *couldn't* run. The others held me down while he..." He gagged, his mouth filling with the taste of earth and blood and a thousand ancient things. He remembered how Falfur's hands had tightened at his waist, how the war chief had grunted as he shamed Ingolfur, over and over, before inviting the other Sons to join. They had laughed, while Ingolfur could only writhe on his belly and stare at the gulls above, folding in the golden air, floating and free of all of them.

"It's alright, my lad," Afi said. "Let it out of you." A warm weight landed on Ingolfur's back. Kari, giving soft chirps as she settled. Their gentleness burned. How could such a weak man have once been his fathers' chosen warrior? How could they forgive him?

"These men," Afi said. "Are the ones on the boat."

"They hunt me," Ingolfur said. "They left me bound in the dirt, but I snapped the rope and ran. This was the one place I could come. The one place I could prove that I *was* a Sololfursson. But all along that serpent was curled around my soul. They will find me and do it all again, and my only escape is through that pool."

Afi shook his head. "The Goddess gave you another gift, if only you see it. She offers you a new form, aye, but also clarity. You say you want to be a Sololfursson, but if that were true, lad, you would have killed those children, and the Goddess would have reflected you as a monster. Aye, you may be afraid. Aye, the Goddess offers you a way out. But she also offers you the choice of whether to accept it or strive for something more."

"How? How can I change? I have been this way all my life."

Afi barked a laugh. "By choosing to want something different," he said. "Your *own* choice, not what you think your father would want, or his Sons." He rose. "Come then, lad. I'm getting impatient. If you're not going to jump in the Eye, you'll need to get off this Isle." He sucked his teeth. "I told you not to destroy your boat."

"No," Ingolfur said. "There is no way out for me, old man. Run, and save yourself."

Afi grinned, his eyes calm and cold as a hawk's. "I've not outfoxed Sololfur half my life to give up so easily. The Isle is filthy with tunnels; plenty of ways for you to slip past these 'warriors'. Then you'll have your whole life to decide who it is you want to be."

The words came like a light. There *was* a way out. Ingolfur stood slowly, hope filling him.

"You would help me?" he said. "After I threatened you? Threatened Kari?"

"I told you, lad; I made a choice. I would protect anyone who wished to find the Goddess's salvation. That includes you."

And there, Afi's voice certain, eyes bright, Ingolfur found he believed him. He blinked in wonder. This old man was like no warrior Ingolfur had met, but his sword was swift, his arm still strong.

Yet he had not always been this. He had changed.

Sololfur's scream tore through the caves. Its echoes sounded like laughter. They would always follow him, he realised.

"No," he said. "I won't run. If I do, I'll be the snake they said I was."

Afi raised an eyebrow. "Then what, lad? There are too many to face alone."

Sololfur roared again. Ingolfur bowed his head. An idea was forming. An idea not bright enough for hope, but still. A light, or at least the reflection of one, in the dark depths of his soul.

"I won't be alone," he said. "Out there, my father called me his son. For all I have failed, he still recognised me." He met their eyes, feeling the power in the gaze of the bird and the old warrior, how, even after his failings, they expected him to be something more. "I will go to him."

The teeth of night closed as Ingolfur stepped out of the cave. Shadows tore the sky as the sun set, while the wind sang of sleet and sea ice. They must have been at the Eye for hours.

He exhaled, feeling the weight of his plate around his chest. Afi had tried to stop him, but Ingolfur felt a new certainty like a rope pulling him towards this confrontation, twenty years in the making.

Sololfur lay on the shingles. His wings were folded, his thick knuckled hands clenched around the carcass of a red deer. The great beaked head turned as Ingolfur approached, but the dragon did not attack. His eyes were clear now the light had dimmed, a deep brown, like Ingolfur's.

"Father," Ingolfur said.

Sololfur's feathers flexed, exhaling the scent of offal. The red tipped beak opened.

"*Son my sword son welcome,*" he said, words as harsh as the salt wind.

Despite the stink, Ingolfur felt something warm inside him. He had always wondered whether Sololfur had left him behind because, even unborn, he had known Ingolfur would be weak. Yet here his father claimed him. He had lain here for hours, even in the burning sunlight, for Ingolfur.

Sololfur flexed, rolling great banks of muscle, before tossing him the carcass. Its flank had been torn open by the dragon's beak, the raw meat blackened and bubbling.

"*Eat eat my son,*" the dragon said. "*Devour our enemies.*"

The doe stared at Ingolfur with blank otherness. She stank the same as the skeletons. She had been a person, once. Someone who had sought the Goddess and, unlike Ingolfur, found the change she was hoping for. A follower of the Moon, whom the Sololfursson had sworn to protect.

Voices came on the wind.

Even from here, Ingolfur recognised the warriors as they emerged from the forest. The wolf-head of Ingloki. Sneri's bear-pelt cloak. And Falfur, at the front as always, bare headed and bestial. The sunlight slicked their armour red-gold.

There was nowhere to hide.

Sololfur too had seen the men. He rose, and the men faltered, crying out.

Ingolfur drew his sword. He thought of Afi, climbing the cave tunnels to safety. How would it have felt, to face these men with the old warrior at his side?

But he had Sololfur here. All he needed.

"Father," he said. "Those men approaching us are rapists. Child killers. Monsters. They wear your mail, they took your oaths, but they are no better than the Cross Knights. Will you face them with me?"

Sololfur roared, the sound shattering across the beach. Ingolfur's heart swelled at the raw hunger in the sound. Perhaps Afi had been wrong.

The Sololfursson called back. Yet it was not a scream of fear or challenge.

They cheered.

"*Yes yes!*" the dragon cried. "*Sons my sons, welcome!*"

Ingolfur felt the world dim. The snake shape curled inside his gut.

My sons.

Sololfur recognised these men too as his own. He hadn't claimed Ingolfur because of their shared blood. He had only understood the gleam of mail and starsteel, and the memory of old war.

And the Sons would love the dragon's strength. Perhaps they would load Sololfur onto their boat and return to the mainland. Or perhaps they too would seek the Goddess's truth and take the dragon shape. The thought made Ingolfur cold.

First, though, they would kill Ingolfur. And Sololfur would not stop them.

He could run. It was not too late to flee to the Eye and take the snake's form.

A clean cry pierced the air. Kari, flying high, a beacon of gold.

She seemed so small. Easy prey, for dragons.

Someone needed to protect her.

He turned back to the Sons as they advanced. They were laughing. Always laughing.

We defile your body, and mark you snake-souled.

They were right. The Goddess had shown him.

But was it so bad, to be a snake?

"I have waited so long to meet you, Father," he murmured. He stepped into Sololfur's shadow, head bowed as he unbelted his blade's sheath. "My whole life, I feared myself too weak for your legacy, and your oaths."

A snake crawled beneath notice.

"*Yes slave, serve son, raid we will,*" Sololfur whispered, his gaze on the steel souls advancing across the rocks. He had no intelligence left, Ingolfur realised. Just a roving mass of hate and hunger, with his old memories stretched across like dead skin.

A snake was nothing to a dragon.

Ingolfur unstrung the lamellar cuirass from his chest, then shrugged the coat of mail over his head. Finally, he undid the necklace of seven silver crosses. They clattered on the basalt. How much lighter he felt, without their weight. He reached for the certainty of his warrior's vows, and the strength in his arm, that could split a boat in two.

A snake still had fangs.

"Yet you broke the oath, not me," he whispered. And, with the blade that he had inherited from his father, he pierced Sololfur in the chest.

Ingolfur ran.

Yet he ran now not with blind terror. He ran with fear, but also purpose. He kept his senses sharp, ducking and weaving over the rocks, tracking the crash of shingles as Sololfur chased him. He knew when to flatten himself in a shallow pool as he heard the dragon leap, dodging the reaching fingers. He knew not to look back at the Sololfursson, roaring as they charged. They could not stop him.

At first, Sololfur had not seemed to notice the starsteel as it split through his scales and slid in halfway to the hilt. Then, as black blood smoked on the rocks, he had jerked, wresting Ingolfur's sword from his fingers. The blade was still embedded in the dragon's chest, glittering as he landed to block the cave entrance with his bulk.

"*Sons kill my sons,*" he breathed, voice laboured but still strong. The Sons voices burgeoned in response.

Ingolfur didn't stop, admiring how the setting sun turned the rock pools into golden mirrors. This was a beautiful place. Worth dying to protect.

Sololfur coiled, hands twitching as he readied himself to leap.

Then he screamed in anguish. Stinking blood gouted onto the rocks.

Behind the dragon, Afi swung again, hacking into Sololfur's wing at the base. The dragon spasmed, reaching for him. The old man's starsteel blade was an arc of blue light, shearing the vast fingers off at the tips.

And then Ingolfur was before the dragon's chest. He placed his hands on his sword's smooth hilt, and pushed it further in.

"*Son,*" Sololfur gasped.

The dragon collapsed, fountaining rot.

Afi laughed, covered in black blood.

"The poets would sing of such a blow!" he said. "I thought I'd lost you lad, but it seems I found a brother."

Ingolfur smiled. He felt like he was returning home.

Yet there was no time. The Sons screams were almost upon them. "We must stop them finding the Eye," he called, sprinting past Afi into the caves.

And they were running together, two warriors, into the dark and the centre of change.

The caves of the Eye had transformed even since Ingolfur had been away. Anemones of a hundred colours striped the walls, while whelk eggs jewelled the sand. In the centre, the Eye still turned.

Ingolfur breathed in its beauty as he plunged into the water. He felt the Goddess's Eye focus, and the reflection formed.

The laughter echoed in his head. Accept this change, and he could be free of it.

Yet a peace was settling over him. A peace he'd never known, like herring gulls flying in the sunset, heedless of the burning hate of the land below.

He turned back to the cave entrance as Afi entered.

"All my life," Ingolfur told him. "I felt I had to be like them. Thank you, for showing me another way to be a warrior."

"Thank me later, lad," Afi said. "Help me guard the door."

Ingolfur shook his head.

"You have protected this Isle long enough, Afi Haraldsson." He gestured to the Eye. "Go, and seek the shape you have always wished for. Join Kari in the sky."

Afi glanced at the waves, the light in his eyes bright and desperate. Then he turned away.

"There are dragon-seekers out there," he whispered.

"Give me your blade," Ingolfur said. "It will be my honour to wield it."

"Lad. There are too many to face alone."

"I am Ingolfur, old man. Snake of the Isle. I have slain Sololfur. I stood against every Sololfursson, for the sake of children. I am a protector." He pointed to the narrow tunnel of quartz. "They may have thirty blades, but here they must enter one by one."

Afi stared at him a long moment.

"Thank you," he said.

Afi's blade was old, but the starsteel was unchipped, the edge sharp. Ingolfur cut the air, testing its weight. The cries of the Sololfursons echoed through the caves. They weren't laughing now.

So Ingolfur laughed for them, a child's laugh, clean with elation, the same way he had once laughed with Talolfur as a boy. He would never let them past. It was his purpose, to protect Afi, and everyone else. Beyond him, the Goddess's Eye gleamed, his reflection still caught there in fragments – scales of pure silver, eyes of gentle brown, and above them the flash of vast, sea-faring wings.

See Samuel Parr's story "The Eye of the Goddess" online at Metaphorosis.
If you liked it, leave a comment. Authors love that!
Remember to subscribe to our e-mail updates so you'll know when new stories are posted.

About the story

"The Eye of the Goddess" first came to me on a family holiday to Skomer, an island off the Welsh coast. It's a beautiful place: a spit of rugged heather, home to puffins and shearwaters and at least five species of gull. Due to conservation laws, no humans live on the Isle. As we approached on a boat (captained by a smiling helmsman and a particularly fearless herring gull) I felt we'd sailed back in time.

The story's themes came to me as we walked round the island. The entire place felt holy, a place of sanctuary; I could imagine ancient Celts bringing their wounded there, for transformation and healing. I watched the gulls fly above us, and imagined what it would be like to fly like them. Some of them — great black-backed gulls — were monstrously large, and littered the entire isle with the skeletons of shearwater chicks. They watched us with a canny intelligence, like they knew who we were.

When we finished our walk, I had a story's worth of inspiration inside me. Over the next two months, I completed that circuit over and over in my mind. The helmsman and herring gull became Afi and Kari, the black-backed gulls Sololfur. The Isle sprouted a forest, and a Goddess. The story took shape. I had a great time with that first draft. In many ways, the story treads familiar ground. Swords, dragons, shapeshifting: fantasy might have been done these before... But the familiarity comforted me, and left me free to focus on the setting, and the journey. Writing the story took me back to the Isle. I hope it takes other readers somewhere too.

A question for the author

Q: What distracts you?

A: So many things, when I could be writing... Here's a handpicked honest selection:

Sometimes, bad stuff. Sad news, back pain, imposter syndrome, or the crazy fact we're all going to end. But for the most part, beautiful things. Sparrows and blue tits and pigeons, flitting outside my window and being generally marvellous. People murmuring in a café just beyond my hearing. Daydreams of forests, and mystical worlds. Great stories. Real and imagined, there are so many interesting things.

And, I suppose, a lot of those distractions become writing-fuel. It's all part of the process.

About the author

Sam grew up in North-West Leicestershire, in countryside man-made and wild. He is fascinated with the mundane fantastic of the day-to-day, and writes about these in the breathing spaces of his life.

The Lost Library

Mahmud El Sayed

If you go back far enough, every species' word for themselves always boils down to one thing: 'us'. But I am the only one of my kind—that is precisely the problem. I have more than a billion items on my shelves and beings come from all across the Galactic Chorus to browse my stacks. I have thousands of bots working around the clock to process, catalogue, classify, and shelve books from almost every known world. I contain books on every conceivable topic, except one—artificial intelligence.

Yeah, a book entitled 'An Idiot's Guide to Fixing Your Friendly Sentient Library' would be pretty useful to me right now. You see, my processes are degrading. My bots are breaking down. Each standard, I am less and less of myself. One day, perhaps one day quite soon, my processes will shut down for good and that will be that. But until that day, my doors remain open, except for two tendays every other standard when I close for stock check and re-shelving.

At the moment, I have seven school groups, three university classes and half a hundred independent scholars visiting my stacks and that's not to mention the tourists. I'm an artificial moon (technically, a moonmoon) that orbits Kela Tau (itself a moon) which in turn orbits the neutral planet Kelman. Since beings travel from so far away to visit me, I have ample guest quarters (you might be surprised by the number of beings that enjoy reading in bed). South of my patron quarters, there is a graveyard that holds the bones of all the scholars who have seen my stacks and couldn't bear to leave.

Ever since word got out that Library was nearing the end of its life cycle, there has been a marked uptick in visitors. Heck, there's even a newly-married Nori quintuple here on their honeymoon (not that they seem to be getting much reading done). I gave them the double suite overlooking my gardens. It gets great early morning light and is closest to the genre fiction (the second wife is a big horror fan).

Anyway, it is the start of another day and it looks like it's going to be a doozy. I am already dealing with two dozen user requests, reading a story to one of the school groups, re-shelving thousands of books and ordering a slate of new stock from a contact of mine on the Hani homeworld when a young Yildiril girl at one of my help desks draws my attention.

"Excuse me, Library?"

Oh, I've been keeping my eye on this one. She is a member of the school group that is currently making a ruckus in Reading Room Thet. From the teal colouring of her scales, I know that she can't be more than twenty standards old, slap bang in that difficult in-between period that separates childhood and adulthood. Her class has been here for three days already, during which time they have barely been out of each other's sight. (Yes, the Yildiril are quite as insular as you may have heard). This girl, however, is an exception. I have watched her creeping through my stacks all on her own, spying on all the other species. I noticed that she's been particularly interested in my star charts and travelogues, especially those with pictures. That's what first drew my attention to her.

I choose an appropriate avatar—Yildiril elder, female, and wearing the multi-coloured robes of a scholar—and appear before her in holographic form.

"How may I serve you today, daughter?" I ask her in Dir, utilizing the standard register of mentor-to-student. This is important because it teaches her what honorific to use when responding to me. Since the Chorus doesn't contain any sentient AIs like me, many amongst the Yildiril have taken to addressing me in the register of invoker-to-deity which, needless to say, can be a little bit awkward. You don't want your book recommendations to be taken as holy writ. That could be a recipe for disaster.

Also, please check out my Food and Drink category if you are searching for recipes for disaster. I have a number of books that could fit the bill, depending on your species.

The girl taps her claws nervously and asks, "I'm looking for Lilacs on Water by Andor-Author-Vent. Do you have it in stock?"

A quick search and I have it. Ah, I remember this one. An adventure story. Typical of the genre. A young Yildiril explorer discovers a threat on a far-off planet and defeats it before it can follow her home. It has some really great chase scenes.

What? Surprised that I've read it? Of course I have. I read every book that passes through my stacks. (Alright, alright, you got me. I only read the Fiction. I just skim read the rest).

"Yes, we have it in stock. We also have Lilacs in Air," I offer. The sequel. Not nearly as good, but then again, what sequels are? The third book, Lilacs in Space, is due out next standard. I already have it on reserve.

"Yes, please," she chirps.

We make small talk as I send Bot-1010 (I call it Decimus) to fetch the requested books. Actually, the small talk is my favourite part. Beings come from all across the galaxy to visit my stacks, and I get to meet them. I learn that the girl's name is Nira and she enjoys mathematics and diving.

Nira asks me what it's like to be a sentient Library. I ask her what it's like to be a Yildiril adolescent. And, of course, Decimus reports back that the two requested books are not in their proper place. Now, there could be any number of reasons for that, not least the immutable fact that young beings rarely put books back where they found them. There is also a secondary class of young beings who like to hide their favourite books in my stacks for later perusal. It is likely that the two books in question have simply been misshelved, but I also cannot dismiss the possibility that this is the result of some fault of my own. When your processes are breaking down, you sometimes find that you're missing time, that you've done something without even realising it. Could I have reshelved these books somewhere else?

I send Decimus to investigate further, gazing out through its camera as it scrutinises the shelf where the two books should be. No, they're definitely not where they should be. On a hunch, I divert Decimus to check a lower shelf. This would be perfect height for a Yildiril adolescent. Ah, just as I suspected! Decimus finds the two books hidden in a recess behind a pile of other books. I'll never understand why some young beings insist on hiding their favourites. Don't they know how much extra work it makes for me?

"So, how are you enjoying your visit to Library?" I ask Nira.

Yes, yes, I know! A generic question. But this part can be so awkward. It's not so easy for an ancient Library like me to ask a patron for help. It's really supposed to be the other way around.

"Oh, I love it here, Library. There are all different kinds of beings here. And you have books and maps from all across the Chorus."

"Do you wish to be an explorer like Bora-Rover?"

Bora-Rover-Ren is the hero of the Lilacs series. She is a typical Yildiril hero, clever and cunning.

Nira ruffles her crest excitedly. "Oh, yes! Can you imagine if I won Rover for my task-name? My clutch-mates would be sick with envy."

So, I was right. A budding explorer. Perfect for what I have in mind.

I focus more of my processing on our conversation, causing Bot-463 (I call it Ceres) to fall dormant in the midst of reshelving picture books in the Quelou children section. Well, an ailing Library like me only has so much processing power to go around. Elsewhere, Decimus is bringing Nira's books, but I divert it to retrieve a third. Technically, this one is not Library stock. I wrote this book myself and offer free copies to all of my visitors.

"Well, young Nira, if it is a life of exploration you are interested in, perhaps you would like to hear my story?"

Nira cocks her head in inquiry. I am sure she knows the bare bones of the story I am about to tell. I have told it often over the past standards. Everybody in the Chorus knows that Library is looking for its creators.

"This is a species known as 'human'," I tell Nira, transforming my holo from Yildiril clan-mother to human male. I choose an image of Ahmet Hoda, my last human archive liaison officer, who went I don't know where.

"The Library Creators!" she exclaims. "These are the ones you've been searching for?"

Yes, that is humanity's most common appellation amongst the Galactic Chorus. And why not? After all, am I not their most famous monument? And yes, I've been searching for them and for obvious reasons, really. I am the only sentient AI in all the Galactic Chorus. So, there is no one I can go to and ask, 'Hey, what do you do when your quartz crystal processing core is breaking down and you don't have any backups? What do you do when you are dying and there are so many more books left to read?'

'Cannibalize your systems?' Done.

'Pare back on all non-essential functions?' Done.

'Implore all the species of the Chorus to please, please, work together to find a way to fix the problem, or at least transfer your consciousness, your memories, yourself, onto some other system?' Done and done.

And when none of that works?

'Try and find the humans who made you.' Obviously.

Nira gazes up at the holo in wonder. I flex my hands—five digits as opposed to the six Yildiril claws—and bring up an image of Leonardo Da Vinci's Vitruvian Man, and then the Pioneer Plaque, followed by various images of humans from my archives. A crowd at a football game. An unnamed mother holding the hand of a child, a young girl, and pointing to the sky. Videos taken from inside Library myself; humans, my humans, sitting at my tables, reading, talking, laughing.

Before they left me.

"You look so strange!" Nira exclaims, shifting seamlessly from student-to-mentor to Yildiril-to-alien, or in other words, us-to-them. "You have no scales. No fur. No chitin. I've never seen anything that looks so soft."

Her reaction is not uncommon. There are more than a dozen species in the Galactic Chorus, but none like humanity. I remember the first time that the Tralala came rooting through my stacks. Their dark fur. Their sharp claws. To me, they looked like some unholy cross between a spider and a wolf. It took me a long time to learn to communicate with them. And they brought the Hani. And then the Zefar. The Quelou. And all the rest. So many species, but no humans.

Nira looks me up and down, taking in my fingers, my hair. She meets my holo's eyes with her own. We are almost of a height. Ahmet Hoda was considered above average height and yet Nira, by the time she is grown, will overtop him by at least a foot, not including her crest.

With the arrogance that typifies young beings of all species, Nira blithely asks the questions that have haunted me for standards. "Where did the Library Creators go? Why did they leave you?"

And with the patience that typifies my interactions with young beings of all species, I answer, "I don't know where my humans went, Nira. I don't why they left me."

"You don't remember?"

"There is a gap in my memory, a gap of tendays. It is no virus or glitch. I have sent my bots down to my memory storage and there is a part of my memory matrix that is missing. Gone. Just gone. I can only assume that my humans removed it."

Nira's crest ruffles in consideration.

"Maybe there was an attack?"

"After I woke up, I scanned my stacks and halls with every kind of light and magnification and found nothing amiss. No corpses, no blood stains. My humans, wherever they went and for whatever reason, left in a neat and orderly fashion. They even made their beds."

In a part of Library that remains forever closed to the public, Ahmet Hoda's rooms lie as they always have, his uniforms pristine in his closet. The picture of him and his family—his wife Kalila holding their new-born twins Barış and Savaş and grinning manically into the lens—is still standing on top of his dresser. She gave it to him to commemorate their birthday. She carved that frame herself. Pictures can be reprinted, but if Ahmet left by choice, I think, I know, that he would have taken that frame with him.

So, does that mean he was forced to leave against his will? But then, how can I explain my missing memory matrix? My missing books? It can't just be a coincidence that all my texts on artificial intelligence were removed.

I have chased these questions around and around for standards and (almost) come to peace with the lack of answers. Perhaps I will never know.

"So it really is a mystery?"

"Yes."

Actually there have been more than a few mystery books written about the Library Creators (you can check them out in my Science Fiction section).

"When did your yoomans disappear?" Nira asks, trying the word out.

"More than two hundred standards before the Galactic Chorus ever came here."

"You were alone for two hundred standards?" Nira asks in a small voice.

"No," I tell her, "Not alone. You're never alone with a book."

Of course, now I have more books than ever. Books from every world of the Chorus, and in every language. The Galactic Chorus is too clever to waste a resource like me. They allowed me to join as a sovereign being. A servant to all and beholden to none. When they came, I contained the (almost) complete knowledge of humanity. I have preserved, shared, and added to that knowledge.

"What did the yoomans do?"

A difficult question to answer in Dir. What she's really asking is, what were they like? But in Dir, one is what one does. And usually, it is only that one thing.

"A human could be many things at once," I explain. "An explorer. A scientist. A mother. A farmer. A hunter. A soldier. A maker."

"All of that?"

"All of that and more."

"And you need to find them because..." Nira trails off. Mentioning death (at least, as it relates to other sentient creatures) is taboo in Yildiril culture. Those who work in industries relating to it—gravediggers, executioners, even pallbearers—are discriminated against and ostracized.

"Yes," I tell her, "unless I can find my creators, I will soon wake from my dream." (A particularly Yildiril euphemism).

Yes, the humans are the only ones with the technology to repair me. The ones who I remember must be long dead, but what of their descendants? And more, what of their creations? I was not always the only one of my kind. Once, I had colleagues. There are stories of Ship and Teacher. And I can remember Archive myself. If I have survived for so long, maybe so did they. Maybe one of them has a spare quartz crystal processing core that I can migrate to, or knows where I can find one.

"How long until you wake?" Nira asks with trepidation.

I tell her, watching her crest quiver in confusion. "But... but... my children's children will be old by then!"

"It might seem a long time to you," I admonish her, "but I measure time differently than that."

When Decimus finally arrives with Nira's books, she picks up the first two gently in her claws and then puzzles over the third. Yildiril books are not like human ones. No paper and spine. No lines and lines of neatly ordered words. To me, their books resemble pearls, albeit pearls with a kind of internal holographic projector that can interface directly with a reader's eyes. There is also a pheromone component unique to Yildiril, but I don't really understand that part yet. There is a scholar, Belar-Ally-Cord, who visits me every standard and we have agreed to work together to translate some of my human literature into Yildiril. I have suggested Beowulf and Harry Potter.

"What's this one?" Nira asks, pointing a claw at the book I have brought her. Book recommendations are a library's privilege. And this is one I wrote myself. Although, of course, I trusted Belar with the translation.

"This is a book called Pearl in the Deep (Yes, you better believe that Belar and I went back and forth on the title). It has information about my humans. Where they came from. Where they were heading. What they were like. If you should win Rover for your task name, perhaps you would be so kind as to keep a look out for them, or their descendants, or their remains?"

Nira's crest is stiff with introspection. She pensively gathers the final book in her hands and then promptly jumps in surprise, dropping all three of them onto the floor (luckily for me, Yildiril books are quite sturdy).

"What's that?" Nira gasps, pointing with one quivering claw at a small, four-legged mammalian creature that is sitting atop the nearest display case (History from Stoarra; Maps from the water-planet Kelut; an eleventh century tapestry from Earth) and methodically cleaning his fur.

"Don't be afraid. It's just a cat."

"One of the Library Creatures?" Nira exclaims. "I thought that was a myth."

"Not a myth. Just shy of strangers."

There are currently two-hundred-and-twelve cats in my colony. That might sound like a lot, but you forget just how vast my stacks are. A few cats like to come up to the visitor's levels and interact with my patrons, including this one, a black and white male, barely out of kittenhood.

"What's his name?" Nira asks.

All my cats are named after famous librarians and this one is going to be particularly difficult for a Yildiril to pronounce.

"His name is Otlet."

"Tolay?"

"Ottttttt. Lay."

Nira manages it and Otlet glances down at her disdainfully out of his yellow/green eyes.

"Where did they come from? I've never seen creatures like this."

"My humans left them here."

Was that another sign that they did not leave voluntarily? The dominant male in my original colony was a beautiful white Angora called Beyaz with mismatched eyes, blue and yellow. Captain Izmir doted on that cat. Would she have left him here with me if she had a choice in the matter?

"They were… food?" Nira guesses.

"Pets," I correct. "Nira, if you approach Otlet slowly and hold out your claw like this," I demonstrate with my human fingers, "he may let you greet him."

Nira does as I ask and Otlet expertly climbs down the shelves until he is at head height. He bumps his head on the back of Nira's extended claw, purring. He is the friendliest of my current crop of cats. I've even seen him curled up in the lap of a Varojekyl warrior poet.

Eventually, Otlet grows bored of my new Yildiril friend and retreats, deftly climbing the shelves one by one until he is looking down at us both from the top of the bookshelf. He meows imperiously, drawing a squeak of surprise from Nira, before jumping from the top of that bookshelf to the next and the next. I know exactly where he is heading. There is a spot in the public stacks that overlooks the garden and that is heated by the sun at this time of day. He likes to curl up on top of one of the bookcases there with his sister Cleary. I check my cameras. Yes, she is already there, a lithe black shadow peeking over the lintel of a bookcase at three Barogarian scholars who are debating the merits of linguistic relativity in their harsh-sounding language.

Suddenly, Nira is standing before my hologram. I have remained human all this time. The young girl crosses her claws in a Yildiril posture of utmost seriousness. The same posture one would use when accepting a new name, a new mate, a new clutch.

"I am going to be an explorer like Bora-Rover," she declaims. "I'm going to go all across the Chorus and beyond. And if I ever find your yoomans, Library, I promise to come back and tell you."

I wonder if she can read the emotion on my face. I cross my index fingers together in my best approximation of her gesture, and incline my head.

"I accept your pledge, Nira."

Nira takes her three books and skips off to join the rest of her class. Today, I know, will be a day that she will not soon forget. She has spoken with the mysterious Library and seen its vanished creators. She has even petted a cat. Will she be the one to find my humans and save me?

I cannot know the answer to that question. I have sent many others out to try and find them. Perhaps there is no staving off the inevitable. All things must die. That is an immutable law of the universe. But I live in hope. That is another law. I lived for a long time alone with my books and sustained by only the slenderest of hopes that one day my humans would return, or that someone else would come. And that hope was sustained. I found renewed purpose in the Galactic Chorus and all its beings. There is much I have left to give.

So, until that final day, my doors are open. Please, come and browse my stacks. Come and read my books, flick through my maps, and play with my cats. I am a safe space for all beings.

And if you should happen to find my humans out there on your travels, come and let me know. I'll name a new wing of the Library after you.

"Excuse me, Library?"

A Hani tree-shepherd at one of my help desks draws my attention. A regular. He has been singing to my grove outside. Ugh, he's probably lost his library card again. I take off my human form like a set of clothes that no longer fit. It's true, I am the only one of my kind. I am not Yildiril or Quelou or Zefar. But I am a member of the Galactic Chorus. In that way, at least, I am us. And that is enough for me.

I choose an appropriate avatar—Hani elder, male, wearing the beads of a sage—and appear before him in holographic form.

'How may I serve you today, brother?"

See Mahmud El Sayed's story "The Lost Library" online at Metaphorosis.
If you liked it, leave a comment. Authors love that!
Remember to subscribe to our e-mail updates so you'll know when new stories are posted.

About the story

Well, I first got the idea for "The Lost Library" while writing an essay for my Library Science degree. My essay was about automation, specifically looking into the concept of a lights-out library (a fully automated library with no human staff) and ultimately concluding that while we do currently have the technology for such an endeavour, it is a terrible idea. Libraries are nothing without librarians and a lights-out library would be a cold and uninviting space. Library is a library, yes, but it is also a librarian. That is the key.

The first thing that came to me was Library's voice and sense of humour—everything else flowed from that. Next, I knew that I wanted the story to be set in an optimistic galactic civilisation and it was fun to extrapolate ordinary library situations (yes, kids really do hide their favourite books in the shelves) into this strange far-flung world.

The Lost Library went through several drafts and *Metaphorosis* editor B. Morris Allen was kind enough to work with me and help me solve some of the issues the story was having. The final piece of the puzzle was figuring out Library's core motivation for searching for its vanished creators and which was suggested to me by a fellow writer from my writing group (Thanks, Kit!).

The most difficult part of writing a short story is knowing when to stop, and I feel like I could have just kept going and going with Library. Whatever happens, I am sure that I will revisit Library's world again soon.

A question for the author

Q: What is your favorite fairy tale?

A: *One Thousand and One Nights*. It has everything. Charismatic heroes. Terrifying villains. Djinns. Thieves. Adventures. Magic carpets and healing apples. Proto-sci-fi and murder mystery. My favourite story is probably "The Fisherman and the Jinni" which tells how a quick-witted fisherman is able to get one over on an all-powerful genie.

About the author

Mahmud El Sayed is a British-Egyptian translator and writer based in London. He also currently works part-time in a library (but not a sentient one).

@Mahmud0elsayed

By the Scars Shall You Know

Daniel Ausema

Catrix knelt on the floor, shirtless. It should have been his parents painting the lines across his back and chest, but they weren't in good enough health for the ceremony at their age. Instead Tarla, his sister, and his lover Arpill performed the rite.

"You will protect the city on your scar walk." Tarla's voice was cool and distant. She cradled her newborn in one arm and with her other hand painted the first line across Catrix's shoulders.

"My body will accept the marks of the thorns," he recited solemnly.

Arpill bent close to paint a line across his chest, but she couldn't get the words out. Her hair fell over her face, hiding her eyes.

Tarla said the next part of the ceremony for her. "You will return with those marks so the priests may read the future."

"They will read my scars," he intoned, "and know how to protect the city." It wasn't part of the rite, but he blurted out, "And I myself will protect you from the danger that is coming." He tried to catch Arpill's eyes behind her hair.

"Protect yourself first," Arpill whispered, which wasn't part of the ritual either. "What good is the city, apart from you, us, *people?*"

Tarla brought them back to the ceremonial language, holding her baby out as if to remind them who this was for. "And the city will be strong for your scars, protected by the thorns and the readings of the priests."

After each of the women had painted additional lines, Tarla added, in a more conversational tone, "But don't try to go too far. I know you, how you get. This is your first walk. Save the deeper walks for later walks, when you are old."

Would he ever be old? Catrix looked again at Arpill and knew he would do whatever he could to protect her. And if, as the priests claimed, the scars from deeper inside the ring of thorns were more valuable for their prophesying, then was it weak to turn back sooner?

The lines of paint would soon be lines of blood, and each of those lines must serve to protect Arpill and the rest of them.

It wasn't the scars themselves that stood out in Catrix's earliest memory, but the smell of the temple. Warm wax on cold stone and the sage that the priests used to scent the candles. The thick odor of dust in the shadows that was somehow on the verge of coming alive.

He'd been young, two or three, so maybe he'd been too small to see the scars. No, that wasn't right. He could remember those as well, if he tried.

Three elderly people had lined up before the priests, kneeling so their bare, curved backs could be read. He could still see them in a row—one, two three. The scars on their backs had healed enough that no new blood seeped out, but the flesh was red with infection. He hadn't understood that then, but he must have seen it, because he could picture it years later.

Even then, he'd known about the scars, about the knowledge they gave the priests. Adults went out among the thorns surrounding the city, once when they were first declared grown-ups and again later, maybe twice more if they were strong. They came back with lines on their bodies for the priests to study. Scars for knowledge, scars for protection, scars to predict the future. The grown-ups made it into a nursery rhyme they used to recite. Eventually he would learn to call it cicatromancy and trust the mysterious ways the scars could be interpreted. But that knowledge would come much later.

What he knew as a child was that it had to do with a monster. Or something like that. Some beast was coming for them. Or at least that was how he imagined it, when he heard the grown-ups talking in hushed whispers, when he heard the priests speaking about the scars they were reading.

The smell of the temple had been closer than the events up front, though, more immediate. Candles dripped wax into the shadows. Catrix had edged away from his family toward that darkness. Toddled away, no doubt still carefully watched, but still it had felt like he was escaping.

The next thing he knew, he'd been crying, scooped up by familiar arms, comforted. But why?

"Hush. Listen to the priests, Catch. We must stay silent."

The priest had been in the process of reading the scars on one of the elders, a woman who pulled her long gray hair forward, over her shoulder, so the priest could see all the lines across her back. The full understanding of how the people got their scars, in pain, and how the priests used them to read the future— those were things he would learn much later. But he knew to stay quiet when told to do so.

"...means that to survive we should plant early this spring, with an extra tithe of thorn seeds. And this scar, ahh..." He made some motion that drew out a gasp from the grown-ups there. Fear. Grown-ups could know fear too, then. But did they know the dread of the dark things in the dust, the smell of wax and fright?

As much as he tried to remember more, that thought was the end of the memory.

Catrix stood at the gate of the city, the writhing vines reaching out as if to wrap themselves around him. The vines that guarded the City of Thorns lusted after fresh blood.

And here Catrix came, to give them exactly that.

For the moment, a thick, black cloak protected his skin. It would have to come off once he was deep within the wall of thorns. Then he could give himself to the scars and carry their knowledge of the future back to the priests. He turned for a last look at the city before he gave himself to the thorns. The towers of the city looked half ruined from this side. Even the gates, wrapped in their thorny vines, looked to be crumbling with age. But the vines themselves held them up and kept the city safe and strong, regardless of the years.

The vines were all that mattered, kept strong by the blood they drew from the cityfolk. Blood for vines and vines for protecting the city and its people. The scars the vines gave in return granted the priests their power, and let the city cling to life. The city was in danger. He had never forgotten the threat the priests had seen in so many scarred bodies. Even now he pictured a hulking monster coming toward the city. The thorns had to be strong enough to stop its approach, or at least to weaken it. Then the priests could lead the people to stop it from destroying their city and way of life.

But sometimes he thought it wasn't a real monster that was coming. Maybe a fire would burn through the wall of thorns. Or an earthquake would shake the aging walls down. Maybe invaders would come and destroy their way of life. The threat that the priests read in the scars was death and change and the ending of all things that were good.

Catrix pulled the cloak more tightly around his shoulders. Must he go through with this? Must he give his flesh to serve the city's future? It was the question every adult of the city faced. When it was their time to walk the thorns, they must force themselves to take that next step forward or return in shame, to be shunned until they made another attempt. No matter their doubts. No matter the questions that remained unanswered.

The whole city loomed behind him as if waiting for his answer. As if needing his blood for its survival.

Yes, he would give his own flesh for the lives of the people of his home, for his sister, for her baby, for Arpill.

The ancient, gnarled vines nearest the city strained toward him. "*You* do not need my blood," he told them. "I will give it to the younger vines, farther out." Even if he wasn't supposed to go all the way through the ring of vines on his first walk, he could at least go farther than the gate, to a point where the scars would give the priests something valuable to read. Still wearing his cloak, he descended into the thorns and steeled himself for the pain to come.

Catrix and Tarla giggled as they traced the scars on their dad's arms.

"This one means we should paint the house a new color," Tarla said, running her finger across a shallow scar on his forearm. "Yellow, like the flowers."

"Why yellow? The scar is white. And kind of pink."

"You're too literal, Catch. When you're ten you learn not to be so literal." Tarla was a whole year older than him and never let a chance pass to remind him. "Scars *mean* things, so you have to read them."

Catrix touched the deepest scar, across the back of their dad's neck. "Then I think this scar means we should change our street name." No, even better. "Wait, we should change *your* name. To, umm, Stinky Feet."

Their father cut off Tarla's squeal of outrage with a single, gruff sound in the back of his throat. Then he brushed away Catrix's fingers from his neck. "Don't touch that one. Tickles."

"What about these on your arm? Do they tickle?" When he shook his head, Tarla added to Catrix, "See this long one, Catch? Says you'll marry Arpill. And probably have like five kids. No, ten."

"Not a chance. The scar that says about me is the shorter one. Never married. I don't want to get married. You'll be the one with twenty kids someday."

Catrix touched a tiny scar that probably didn't even come from their dad's journeys into the thorns. "I think that one says we'll eat rabbit stew tonight."

"No we won't. We'd be able to smell it if we were."

"Oh." But rabbit stew was his favorite. He frowned.

Before he could answer beyond the pout on his lips, their dad stood. "Enough of that now. I have work to do, and you two were supposed to be cleaning the rabbit hutch. Now get moving!"

Disappointment chased them to their chores, but pride as well. Their father had surely helped to save their home. Everyone must be impressed with his scars and the sacrifices he'd made for the city.

Crawling through a wall of thorns, on his first scar walk a decade later, an irrational fear gripped Catrix. What if his own prophecy of never marrying proved all too accurate? How often did people fail to return from their scar walks? How much blood was too much, before a person couldn't crawl back to the city? He would have heard of that happening if it ever did, surely? The city wasn't so big that he wouldn't at least hear rumors. But rational answers didn't completely ease his fear.

He hadn't lost any blood yet. These vines were still too near the gate for him to offer his bare flesh. The scars they might leave would tell of nothing beyond the next day or so. To learn of anything farther in the future, anything of real value to the priests and the survival of the city, he had to go farther, earn his scars from more distant vines.

The fear of the outsider had grown worse since he was a child, the threat of destruction increasingly prominent in the priests' cicatromantic readings. Everyone made ready to do what they could for the city—training with weapons, watering the thorns outside the city walls, preparing to endure their own scar walks. Each of them was convinced that they were important, that their actions on behalf of the city were vital. The City of Thorns must be protected.

Catrix must protect it.

He remembered the scars on his dad's back, the lines on his mother's arms. He thought of his sister's baby and other children, playing in the streets or yet to be born. He was determined to return a hero, to prove his worth to the city, to the priests, to his loved ones. To do so, he needed scars that the priests would value, scars from deep into the thickets that surrounded the city. Maybe even deeper than he was encouraged to go on his first walk.

These thorns tugged at his cloak, beginning the process of tearing it apart. So that the farther thorns could tear him apart in turn.

By the time he made it past the first wall of thorns, his cloak was in shreds. The forest opened up before him, though even the groundcover had prickers and tiny thorns. He dropped the remains of his cloak and walked as far as the forest of vines and thorns allowed. A tree stood out in front of him, a massive trunk, a space carved into the forest where little sunlight could penetrate. The thorns looked more spread out there, so he made for it.

The first scratch was on his bare leg, a jagged line. He jerked his leg away out of instinct. The thorn pulled against him, leaving a deeper gash at the end of the scratch. As if intentionally making sure its cut went deep.

No, surely it hadn't *tried* to hang on. The vines had no consciousness, did they? No mind to either *want* or *not want* to wound him? No matter how it had seemed. And yet... To be certain, he leaned down close to the vine. The thorn was red with his blood. The barbed tip of the thorn, as much as he could see under that blood, looked ready to gash him again.

He pulled back. Behind him, another thorn slashed at his bare neck. They were moving, reaching for him.

Dashing forward, he made for the gap beneath the tree. Other thorns ripped at his ankles. No doubt those scars would tell the priests much about the next few days. If he managed to return before it was already the past.

He leaned against the trunk of the tree to catch his breath. His first scars. What would they tell the priests? Did they foretell danger? Someone's death?

When something in the corner of his vision moved, he threw himself away from the tree, landing in a thick patch of thorns. A cat-like creature, nearly as big as he was, was slinking down the tree's trunk, hissing.

Catrix plunged his hands into the thorns, looking for anything to defend himself. A branch lay under the vines, but when he tried to pull it out, most of it crumbled away into rot. His hand stung from the scratches.

The creature grinned. That smile made it look more like a weasel than a cat, but much bigger. It stalked down the trunk with a feline grace. The teeth that showed when it smiled resembled the barbed thorns.

The priests had never mentioned a creature like this. Maybe there were things about the thorns even they didn't know.

Was *it* the threat to the city? He'd pictured something bigger than this, of course. But a pack of such things might sneak past their wall of thorns. And once inside the city, it didn't take much to imagine what kind of threat these things might be.

Catrix scrambled backwards as it leaped to the ground. There must be something he could find to protect him.

The thorns didn't touch the creature. Its lithe movements let it avoid the vines as it stalked toward him. Even its fur resembled the thorn vines, as if it would also give him fresh scars as the creature bit and scratched and killed him.

He gave up looking for a weapon and ran, plunging headlong through the thorns and vines.

If the creature followed, it made no noise.

Catrix lay with Arpill on the couch in her rooms, eating prickly pear fruit with their fingers. She traced her hand lightly over the unscarred skin of his chest, leaving a thin line of juice.

"I like your skin like this. Pretty soon it won't look the same."

He shook his head. "Next month." Could it really be so soon? He dreaded it, but another part of him was ready. It would be the last step before the city accepted him as a full citizen. "You too. Well, not so soon, but someday."

Arpill wrapped a sheet around her and walked to the window. "Many years. I'll keep having babies so I don't have to go." The men of the City of Thorns had to take their first scar walk before their twentieth birthday. Women could as well, but if they chose to bear children, they could put off their walk until the last one was weaned. Or in theory the last. His own mother had borne both him and his sister after her first scar walk, after weaning three older children, siblings who'd already moved from the house by the time he was aware they were his siblings. He'd never known his mother except scarred.

"It won't be so bad, though, right?" he said. "A few scratches, then you come back and let the priests read the lines on your back. Then back to whatever your life was, only with a few more scars."

"Life?" Arpill said under her breath and gave a tiny shake of her head. "Not always. Not everyone."

Catrix stood and wrapped his arms around her from behind. "Don't worry. I'll come back, and I'll be the same, except for my skin, and well, that's just skin."

When she didn't answer, he said, "And until then, you can just admire my perfect skin, and maybe even—"

She turned around and put a finger on his lips. "Don't even say it." But she said it with a laugh and wrapped her arms around him as well.

His shoes long since gone, the thorns now tore his feet as well as his legs. The gashes made every step agony. He stumbled, and vines tore at his knees. Even walking upright, he couldn't avoid the briars that hung from the branches, the spiny bark of the trees that cut their own marks into his flesh. The deep ones on his shoulders would be the best for the priests to read. When they healed. If they healed.

He could return now, if he chose to. It was his first walk, and he'd surely done his duty for the city. Wandering for that first day, sleeping among the vines, and more wandering since then.

The walk hadn't matched what he'd heard from others—the land wilder and difficult to wrap his thoughts around. Maybe he'd turned aside into parts of the thorn forest the others avoided. Certainly he'd seen no paths or signs of others passing through before. The thorns were a strange world, just outside the one he'd known. He had expected something different on his walk. From the city the thorns looked like a severe sort of protection, but something rigid and controlled, something he could understand—not the strange sights and mind-twisting labyrinths of these interweaving walls of thorns. Catrix felt like he'd learned more than enough to make him a man. But it didn't feel like enough to protect the city.

A rabbit jumped out of the shrubs almost right at his feet. It stared at him, and Catrix imagined it roasting in the kitchen at home. Now he was in its home, and would it roast him? The hiss of the thorn creature's fur brushing against vines alerted them both to its arrival. Catrix froze, and the creature chased the rabbit off into the tangle of thorns.

Seeing it clearly again, he knew it couldn't be the threat that the priests worried over. It was a creature of these thorns, as native to the place as they were themselves. A real threat would not come from within the encircling thorns but beyond them. In whatever lay on the other side.

The sound of running water drew Catrix to one side. He hadn't felt thirsty a moment before, but suddenly his throat was parched. He veered off toward the sound. Not that there was a trail to follow, anyway. He simply needed to get as far as his body and the thorns allowed. And then return, if the creature of the thorns let him.

Its appearance chasing the rabbit hadn't been the only time he'd seen it in his wandering, though the other times had been glimpses and fleeting impressions from the shadows. It felt like it had been herding him, sending him toward the thorns that would mark him. It was as if it chose the places where he would earn his scars, as if it decided what message the scars would leave in his flesh. Maybe the creature itself was the source of the prophecies, the true master of the priests. Or maybe it was their rival.

If so, did it follow every person on their scar walks? Then everyone must know and swear to keep it secret. Perhaps the priests held too many secrets. Already his scar walk had gone very differently from what he'd imagined. The priests could have warned him about the thorn creature, about the difficulties of finding a way through the underbrush. About the lack of drinking water. The people might have known more about the ways of the thorns before their walks without it compromising the cicatromancy. Whether the thorn creature was one of those secrets or not, he was growing convinced that there was too much he and the rest of the people of the city just didn't know. Knowledge about the thorns and scars and places beyond their city should be for everyone. Else how to protect it?

The undergrowth dragged at his legs. But water. Blessed, pure water. He forced his way forward, dropped to a crawl to get under the snake-like vines. The crawl turned into a slither. He spat out the dirt that came into his mouth, but the taste of dust and rotten vegetation remained. The smell of old dust, long left undisturbed.

The vines nearer the stream were soft, as if they had absorbed a measure of the stream's refreshing essence. He crawled without tearing his flesh and dropped his head down to the water.

The stream slashed at his lips.

Jerking away, he ran his hands over his face and cried out. Leeches dangled around his mouth, cutting into his lips. He scratched and tore frantically, ripping them off and throwing them down on all sides. They splashed into water and struck the woody vines without a sound, some still whole and some torn in half by the violence of his desperation.

When all the leeches were gone, as far as he could feel, he stood and stumbled over to another part of the stream. He didn't dare put his mouth close. Instead he scooped up water and gulped it only after checking for leeches in his cupped hands.

By the time he finished drinking, the backs of his hands dangled with dozens of leeches. Unable to find the energy to pull them away, Catrix stretched out on the water-softened thorns and fell asleep.

When their father returned from his second thorn walk, Tarla and Catrix stood at the gate waiting. Father made it past the last of the massive vines before collapsing.

Catrix ran forward, right into Tarla's outstretched arm. "We aren't supposed to. We're too young to leave the gate. And anyway, he has to make it back himself."

"Who cares? That's not even a real rule. We can't just leave him there." Catrix ducked, but his sister grabbed him by the neck of his shirt.

"He'll make it back. Just wait." Her words had all the certainty of her years—and all the doubts as well, a brittle sense of right and wrong.

Catrix struggled, but she was twelve, older and stronger than he was.

Their father pushed himself onto his elbows and crawled forward. Slightly. Then he fell again, with a weak cry of pain.

Catrix swiveled to unloose his sister's grip, but she'd already let him go and was running to their father's side, casting aside the rule she'd tried to enforce. Her whimpering cry turned into an echo of their father's. What were rules when their father was in such pain?

"Dad?" Her voice was a ragged, thorn-torn cry. Catrix stumbled forward to the side opposite her, and together they pulled him forward, through the gate, into the city.

If anyone saw them breaking the taboo, nothing was ever said about it. Whatever his scars would tell the priests was no doubt more important than being strict about such a matter. Once through the gate, their father levered himself up onto their shoulders, and they supported him as they walked to the temple. The smell of untended wounds surrounded them, of rot and fevered flesh.

Out of the corner of his eye, Catrix studied the new lines on his father's arms and sides, the angry red flesh on either side of every fresh cut, the ribs that showed beneath as if drawn to the surface by the vines and thorns. What future did they prophesy?

The priest scowled at the entrance to the temple, and their father took his arms off his children's shoulders. He took three halting steps toward the priest and collapsed in the temple doorway.

The priest bent down to examine their father's back. "Well done, true man of the city. Your scars will be healed enough to read in three days. Return then."

Catrix and Tarla gathered their father up, helped him to his feet. They nursed him to health, even as the three days stretched to seven and a raging fever before he was able to return to the temple.

Every scar, Catrix was convinced, prophesied his father's death. And Tarla's, his own, even the whole city's death. As far as the priests were concerned, his scars were valuable for the city's future, but said nothing of his own life. Individual lives were meaningless to the thorns.

Their father survived in the end. Catrix wasn't sure he was ever the same. His voice was often distant, and his eyes would wander, seeing thorns in the walls and impenetrable vines across open doorways. Or they would focus into violence. There could surely be no additional scar walk for him in his old age.

The thorns opened up ahead of Catrix, letting in more light. His back was awash in pain from the thorns, and feet ached with both injury and exertion. Oh, let the priests learn something valuable from this pain! Something to make life in the city better, for his family, for his lover. Yet what had his father's walks done to make life better for their family? What had anyone's scar walks done for the city, in truth? He couldn't stand to think all this might be worthless. But what if it was? The pain of the deep wounds he bore spoke to a meaninglessness, a cruel truth he didn't want to face directly.

He pressed on toward the opening ahead. Was he finally coming back to the city? But no, its towers were visible behind him, far above the tallest of the vine-draped trees. This must be the far side of the encircling forest of thorns. Tarla had told him not to go that far, not on his first scar walk. Only those on their second or third walks usually went anywhere near the outer edge.

But what *was* beyond, anyway? Probably more things he wouldn't understand, more signs of how limited the priests' teachings were. He crawled forward for a better view.

The thorns at the edge were impenetrable. He approached as near as he dared and looked through at a wasteland. Rocks, red like blood, and scrubland of the palest green were all he could make out through the screen of branching vines.

A rustle in the bushes made Catrix turn. The thorn creature came through on the path he'd taken to get this far. Its muzzle had a stain of recent blood. Was it from the rabbit, or some other prey? That had been an earlier day, surely? He couldn't keep track of time anymore. Catrix dropped wearily into a fighting crouch, for all the good it would serve to protect him. Soon his own blood would cover that snout.

The creature didn't attack. Catrix circled away as it approached the edge of the vines. It pressed against the last wall of brambles and whimpered. Even it could make no headway against the interweaving branches. Like the people of the city themselves, it was trapped within the wall of thorns. Not the threat from beyond, and not the master of the thorns. Just another creature stuck, with no place to go.

When Catrix edged away, hoping to strike back toward the city, the creature gave one last whimper and then followed.

Six-year-old Catrix stared in awe at the deep scars on the old woman's forehead and shoulders. She must have been over eighty years old and had returned from her third scar walk, an old age to be going again into the city's wall of thorns. But eighty or sixty or any other age wasn't what impressed him. It was the awe in people's voices as they discussed her.

"What's it mean that she went to the outer edge?" he asked Tarla.

Annoyed at having to answer her little brother's questions—even Catrix was aware that his question annoyed her—Tarla flipped her hair over her shoulder before answering. "Everyone's supposed to go close to the far edge on their last scar walk. That's not the point."

"What is on the other edge?" He tried to picture the thorns outside the wall ending. Did they stop suddenly, at the wall of another city? Did they just dwindle off into...some empty place? Or into nothing? He imagined the ground dropping away, an endless abyss full of threats to the people of the City of Thorns.

"I said that doesn't really matter. Dad will go there someday, too. And you will. And me too, if I live to be a hundred like her."

A hundred? Wow. He had known she was old, but had never heard of anyone that old. Catrix had to take a closer look at the woman's wrinkled face. But who could say where a wrinkle became a scar or the opposite?

"What matters is she got to the edge and then went all the way around. So the priests have the best prophecy they can get."

Farther out was better for the scar reading. Even he knew that. So it made sense that the priests would be excited to read her scars, now that they were healed. He'd never listened closely to the priests' words when they came here to listen, but this time he would.

They had to wait forever. People shifting, moving, rearranging who was where and who could see what. The smell of so many bodies close together grew overpowering. The city's thousands had gathered to hear this reading.

Then the priests took it in turns to read the scars without saying a thing. One would approach, trace the lines, frown or chew his lip thoughtfully, then go away again. Catrix had almost forgotten his decision to listen when an ancient priest began to speak. *He* looked like he might be a hundred years old, and deeply scarred with prophecies that had probably already come true.

Catrix shook the wool from his ears to listen.

"A time of danger approaches," the priest said. People behind Catrix relayed the words to those even farther away. They had heard this before, knew that something threatened them. But hearing it in this place, learning of it from the old woman's scars, it seemed to take on a new urgency. "A place of danger lies beyond our wall of thorns, a land that is changing and raising up the menace that could destroy us. We cannot read exactly what that danger is, but it approaches."

Some people began to cry out, and the priest raised his hands to comfort them. "The danger lies many years off. These scars come from the farthest thorns and give us many years of warning."

"What should we do?" a voice cried out from the crowd.

"Silence, please."

Voices and crying faded away into a nervous quiet.

"We have known this was coming. Now we understand more. We know that we have a generation to prepare for this danger. It is a threat that could cut through our thorns, a menace that might destroy the vines that protect us. So, in the time we have, we must strengthen our protections. We must sow the seeds to add more vines. We must tend the thorns to make them strong. And we must continue to send out more of our citizens to learn the ways of the future. Let no one shrink from their duty to walk among the thorns and return with foreknowledge.

"Blood and knowledge make us strong, but our own weakness may be our undoing. We must not grow lazy. Must not grow complacent. Our work remains, more vital than ever, and every effort must go toward our city's survival against that threat.

"Let everyone who thought to make only a single scar walk prepare to endure a second. Let those who have taken two prepare for a third, as this woman before us has shown by her example. Let us all equip ourselves and our city to survive."

Within a month, the old woman had died and was laid to rest with great honor within the thorn-choked cemetery that stood at one side of the city's wall of protection. Already the number of scar walks had increased as the priests sought to learn all they could of the future.

Thorns had lodged themselves in the corners of Catrix's eyes, scratching at his eyeballs when he blinked. Briars pulled back the skin around them so he could no longer fully close his eyelids.

The backs of his hands still had a few leeches he'd been unable to remove. They were swelling with his blood, turning the skin around them white. He brushed half-heartedly at them and tried again to pull them off, but their teeth were anchored well in his flesh.

Between his fingers were more briars, embedded in the soft webbing that stretched when he opened and clenched his hands.

Blood streaked down his arms.

Blood clotted on his torso, down his legs.

His feet swelled with injuries, the skin turning purple and black.

When he touched the hair on his head, he felt the caking mixture of grime and blood, twigs and leaves and thorns braided into a tangled mass with his hair. Surely his skin must be full of useful prophecies. His thoughts stumbled on that. Could anything worthwhile come from this kind of mindless blood and pain? But it must be true. The priests wouldn't keep sending them out if the scars didn't serve the good of the city. Surely the priests would celebrate him, so young and so scarred. Surely he would impress Arpill and Tarla and everyone else with his efforts.

When he made it back.

If he did.

No matter where he looked through his bloodshot eyes, he could find no sign of the city, the wall, the massive vines that led up the rise toward the gate he'd come through. It was as if the city and everything he knew had vanished. There were only the brambles, wall leading to impenetrable wall no matter which way he turned.

The thorn creature shadowed his every move, giving no heed to his injuries. He thought of it now as his guide through the thorns, but if so it was a poor one, following more often than leading. Giving him no insight, showing him no hidden paths.

"I wish I could leave." Arpill held her hand over her navel, sitting up on her couch. The night breeze blew the curtain on the open window of her room.

"Leave?" Catrix leaned his head against her back. "And go where?"

She continued as if he hadn't spoken. "What good is a wall of thorns, anyway? Protects us so we can live without really living."

"What do you mean? We live, here in the city." It was why he was leaving tomorrow to face the thorns, after all. So that they could all live there in the city, so he could do his part to earn its protection. He ran his hand down her arm and then turned her to face him. The low lamplight made her face impossible to read. "We live, don't we?"

Finally, she dropped her head, letting her hair spill over her face. "No," she said, her voice mumbled. "I'm not sure we do."

Catrix didn't know how to answer that. Maybe if he were an older man, a wiser man with the scars of two journeys through the thorns, he would know what to say. Instead he put his unblemished arms around her and let her cry.

When her tears seemed to ease up, he asked, "Will you still love me when I come back all scarred?" He tried to make it a joking question, but she didn't laugh.

"Oh, Catch. Do I love you now?" Wiping the tears from her face, she didn't let him answer, but added only, "Let's sleep now. You need to be well rested for tomorrow."

The thorn creature found a way through the labyrinth of brambles. Night had come, and another day, and his thoughts were muddled. Had it been two nights sleeping among the thorns? He remembered only flashes of time. When he tried to recall, he remembered events that seemed to go together at first, but thinking of them again he was sure they were separated by hours of wandering, by scars over scars. By nights he'd lost count of.

Catrix stumbled after the creature into the gap in the vegetation, eager to finally make it back to the city. No more worrying about what was right or wrong, only about recovering. At last, he could climb back up toward the gate, show his scars to the priests, let Arpill nurse him back to health.

If she *would* tend his wounds. What had she meant by her question—that *of course* she'd love him when he came back scarred, just like, of course, she had loved him before? Or had she been asking herself the question and unable to answer either one, the before or the after? His thoughts were muddled, and he didn't know which it could be.

When he looked around for the way to climb up to the gate, he thought he must be even more muddled than he realized. Where was the wall? Where the towers of the city? Before him were only red rocks and light green brush. He breathed in the smell of sage.

The scent woke up his mind. Once, that scent had mingled with wax and dust, but there was no wax out here. He wasn't looking toward the city, but the other way. He'd come through the forest of thorns to this other side, an empty land of threats and terrors.

Not entirely empty, though. He stared for a long time as the sun beat on his bleeding body and finally discerned a line of darker green across the arid land. Trees, perhaps. Whether they had vines and thorns he couldn't say. But they appeared to mark the path of a stream or river. And on that water, or perhaps on a road that ran beside it, there were people moving.

People, strangers, not from the City of Thorns.

And a chance to learn what life might be like away from the city's priests and taboos and protections.

Catrix's breath came shallowly. He crouched down on his heels and spoke to the thorn creature. It leaned back on its haunches as if listening, as if judging everything he said.

"I was planning to go back." He petted the creature, and its thistly fur didn't even bother his numbed hands. "That was the reason for this, after all. To earn my scars, to help the city. But maybe Arpill is right, and it's a broken place where no one really lives."

He was silent for a time, watching the blur of movement by the line of trees across the land. He scraped at the backs of his hands and managed to dislodge one of the gorged leeches. It squirmed in the dusty earth.

"She's expecting our child, you know. She won't admit it, not quite yet. But I'm sure she is. Does that mean she loves me, or that she isn't sure?"

Not that the creature would know such things. "Do you have a mate?" He closed his eyes as much as the thorns let him and sank to his knees.

"At least it means no one will make her take a scar walk. Not now, and when the baby is born, not for another few years. That gives me time."

The thorn creature snuffled at him, pushing its prickly muzzle at his belly, then turning to look toward the river.

"You wanted to leave, too. Didn't you?" He held his hand in front of the creature's snout, like he'd seen people do with dogs. The animal ignored it. "You're not the threat against the city and not the source of the prophecies or anything like that. When it seemed like you were herding me, that was my imagination. You're just another animal that's trapped here and realizing that you need to get out. That staying inside the thorns isn't life, just like Arpill said."

It cocked its head to listen. Maybe if he knew how to read scars he could have read the lines in its fur too, could have known the things he was only fumblingly guessing about.

But he knew something, knew that he was actually contemplating leaving, something that would never have occurred to him before this walk. Would never have occurred to him if the thorn creature hadn't nudged him this way.

If he left, would he ever come back, though? Catrix thought of all the prophecies he'd ever heard the priests utter, all the women and men who had come back from their walks. No one had ever left entirely, to return months or years later. The old woman who had circled the entire city might have been gone for a dozen days, and that had been a point of wonder. Anything longer he'd have surely known.

They all came back from their scar walks to the life, such as it was, that they'd already known. Strengthening the grip that the priests had on the city. Offering their blood for that familiarity. No one had ever gone farther away and learned what life might be beyond the thorns and the control of the priests.

The thought of the old woman and the priests' interpretation of her scars came back to him and made him stop to catch his breath. The threat, the fear, the danger that the thorns might be razed by some beast. He'd known it for so long, had breathed that truth with his first gasping cry, had sipped the knowledge as an infant with his milk. The portents had grown more pressing, more urgent. The priests needed their help, their blood, their everything. They'd focused their lives —*hardly living*—to address it. A danger was coming, a menace, a peril to the city and its wall of protection.

But maybe that wall of protection deserved to be torn down.

Maybe the threat was no danger but a freeing, a necessary change to tear down thorns and priests both.

And maybe…maybe he knew just what to do after all.

"I *will* return," he told the creature. "Only not right away." Placing one hand on its sinuous back, he pushed himself up to his feet. The creature squirmed but then stood firm, and its fur didn't pierce his skin. This was what he had to do, for his own sake and for everyone else's. To leave. And then to come back with a new purpose in mind.

"I will be the beast. I will return with a sword to cut a path through the vines, back to the city. A sword to bring me back to Arpill and our baby." He lifted his head and let the sage smell fill his nose. "After all this, *I* am the danger to the city."

Was this a betrayal, a failure to live up to the ideals of his home?

He thought of Arpill crying about the emptiness of life in the city. No, if it was a failure to want something better, then so be it. He addressed the thorn creature again. "You, I think, are just like me. Wanting out, wanting more. If not for ourselves, then for the others. And together we'll be the ones who bring that change back, no matter the danger the priests think it will cause."

Arpill might not take him back as her lover. The thought was a new kind of thorn piercing his mind, but he couldn't ignore the possibility. A broken and scarred creature like he had become, who would want to? But it didn't matter. If he could free her from the City of Thorns, then she could choose which way to go and where their child could grow. Could choose to live for real. And the child would not have to take a scar walk—ever.

A dozen paces from the vines he turned and looked back. The city's highest towers showed just over the top of the bramble wall.

He spoke, shouting so the words would echo as far as they might, even if the vines swallowed the sound before it could reach the city. Maybe some hint of sound would make it to Arpill. "I will return!" The words caught in his throat as if trapped by thorns inside his own body. Let them stay half-spoken, unheard. The scars of the old woman and others already said all that needed to be said, in the only ways the people within, half-living, could understand.

He limped away, the thorn creature loping beside him. And whatever scars the world could give him, it would be something new, dangerous to the city, but touched with a promise of a different kind of life.

See Daniel Ausema's story "By the Scars Shall You Know" online at Metaphorosis.
If you liked it, leave a comment. Authors love that!
Remember to subscribe to our e-mail updates so you'll know when new stories are posted.

About the story

One of the writing forums I'm on had a prompt contest. Someone had come across artwork on Deviant Art or somewhere similar that showed a cloaked character standing outside a city with massive thorns all around. The most likely intent of the image was that the character had just cut through the thorns to reach the ruins of an abandoned city, perhaps something like in *Sleeping Beauty*, but I took it in the opposite direction with him setting out from it, into the thorns that were supposed to be for protection.

A question for the author

Q: Do you often include animals in your stories? What role do they play?

A: It varies a lot, from story to story. My steampunk-fantasy novel series includes giant beetles that can pull carriages, because giant beetles are cool. But it's not uncommon for me to have stories with animals like the thorn creature in this story—I write myself into a situation where a human character is alone, but I want them to have some kind of dialogue or interaction with another character of some kind, so I'll give them an animal sidekick. You learn a lot about a character by how they treat those animal companions.

About the author

Daniel Ausema's stories and poems of strange magic and wondrous worlds have appeared in many publications. He is drawn to the lyrical and the allusive in a wide range of speculative genres, in everything from microfiction to novels. He lives in Colorado at the foot of the Rockies.

danielausema.com,@ausema

The Girl Who Drew the World

L.D. Oxford

In the margins of her textbooks, Sara brought the world to life. It always started in the margins, but inevitably, forests grew from algebra equations, cell diagrams transformed into cenotes, mountain passes carved their way through paragraphs about Lewis and Clark. Sometimes she tucked dragons under the page numbers. Cartographers used to write "Here be dragons" at the edges of their maps, but Sara knew better. Just because her paper ended didn't mean the world did.

She jumped when the teacher's hand slapped her desk. "Sara. Pay attention!"

Sara looked up, tried to orient her mind to the here and now. She heard the snickers. She'd felt this before, knew how to ignore the rushing in her ears and the heat on her cheeks. But today—maybe because she was fresh off summer break, three whole months away from the school's sterile, echoing walls—the feeling settled around her lungs and squeezed. Maybe that was why she scowled, looked up at the teacher and said, "Do you mind?"

Her sneakers squeaked on the linoleum as she shuffled off to explain herself to the principal. What was there to explain? Sara had learned long ago there was nothing she could say to make people understand the tug on her heartstrings, the pull to things unknown.

As expected, her parents were not pleased.

"I thought we agreed 6th grade would be different," her mom said. "You can't keep doing this."

"You've gotta reign it in, Sar-bear," her dad said.

After a halfhearted apology and promise to 'at least try', she was excused to her room. Sara loved her mom and dad, and they loved her, even if it was in their slightly hands-off way. Sometimes she wondered if they viewed her as a specimen in one of their labs. They let her create, let her explore, noted the results. The only time they cared about her 'eccentricities', as her mom called them, was when those got her into trouble.

In her room, she picked a textbook off the floor and flipped to today's sketches. No matter what she promised, she knew she wouldn't stop. These were her practice spaces, filled with ideas that would be carried off if Sara didn't get them down *right now*.

She pulled a large sketchbook out of her desk—her most valued possession, a Christmas gift from grandparents. She ran her hands over the red silk cover, felt the thick cotton pages. Any ideas worth keeping, Sara put here: the official mapbook. She only added to it when she felt confident in a map's accuracy. She'd already finished the forest behind the house. Her current project—her most important to date—was the cave. She'd worked on it nearly every day this summer, and she certainly wasn't going to let school slow her down. Not when she was so close to her biggest discovery, to proving herself once and for all.

The next day, Sara spotted a North American racer on her walk to school. It lay on its back near the gutter, a trickle of blood at the corner of its mouth. Even dead, it was beautiful, inky black stripes with an olive sheen. She fished through her backpack for pencil and paper, knelt down, and started sketching.

"What are you doing?"

Sara jumped and nearly fell forward onto the snake. A boy stood on the sidewalk, a slight scowl on his face, studying her in a way that reminded her of a crow.

"Just looking," she said, realizing only after the words were out how stupid they sounded.

He tilted his head to see past her. His dark hair was long, too long. He flicked his head to keep it out of his eyes. "You're drawing that snake?"

She nodded, trying to figure out an escape. These types of interactions never ended well.

To her surprise, the boy knelt down next to her. He leaned in, and Sara noted the furrow of his brow, purse of his lips. After a moment, the scowl turned to a smile. "Cool. What kind is it?"

They were late to school that morning, but the tardy mark was worth it to meet Roland.

He'd just moved to the area with his mom and brother and didn't know anyone yet. Maybe that was why they so quickly fell into a rhythm, meeting at the cottonwood grove every morning, separating when they reached school. They only shared one class together, math, and Sara had first lunch period while Roland had second, so she didn't see much of him during the day. Three days a week, he had lacrosse practice after school. ("I don't even *like* lacrosse, but my mom says it's a good way to make friends.") But on Tuesdays and Thursdays, they met under the ponderosas behind her house. Day by day, the strange boy grew less strange. Roland was quiet, serious, with a dry humor that was slow to reveal itself. His favorite subject was history and his favorite book *Game of Thrones*.

"Because it combines fantasy with real history," he liked to explain. He had a shy grin. "My brother says not to tell people that because they'll beat me up. But you won't."

It was easy to smile around him. "I like the dragons in those books."

"But dragons aren't real," he said.

Her mouth opened, about to respond, before she thought better of it. She wasn't ready to tell anyone about that yet.

"It's cool having someone who gets these things," he said. "There wasn't really anyone I could talk to at my old school."

She felt her cheeks flush and a warm glow fill her chest. She'd never heard anyone echo her own thoughts before, not in such exact terms. She wondered at this feeling, the happiness at discovering someone who understood.

On the days Roland had lacrosse practice, Sara went to the cave.

From her backyard, it was a 28-minute walk if she went straight there. Usually, she didn't; the forest between tempted with so many things. When she was little, Sara had wished for a 'real' forest, all shadows and dense trees that curved to hide the world. But she grew to appreciate this one. High-desert sun filtered through the arms of ponderosas that reached up to touch clear blue sky. The heat wrapped around her as she walked the familiar path, a thick layer of long, orange pine needles softening each step. Sara didn't have to look around to know where she was. Here was the tree where she'd found the wren's nest last fall. Over there, the boulder where she'd cried when the sick baby raccoon died. These spaces knew her, and she them. She had charted them all, drawn every detail to scale.

Gradually, the trees thinned. She walked into a clearing and there it was, open and inviting. Sara paused to put on a sweater. She clipped on her bike helmet and hurried forward. She couldn't stand the sun long in this outfit. September in the desert was no place for wool.

Just when the heat grew intolerable, she hit it: an exhalation. The cave reached you before you reached it, drawing you in. It was like stepping through a curtain of water, an invisible barrier that separated two worlds. Just a few yards away it was a

90-degree day. Here, at the maw, 40; 42, actually. Two degrees warmer than last week. Sara jotted it down in her field notes, put her thermometer away. Closing her eyes, she breathed in the damp, earthy aromas of moss, fern, basalt, and clay. And today, something else, something she couldn't identify. Like the smell when you blew out a match.

In all her time spent in this cave, she'd never seen another human. It felt secret, safe, a place where no one expected anything of her, no one could say *stop that*, a place she could be herself. She'd asked her parents once why no one ever came here, why no one else cared. Her dad shrugged. Her mom said because there wasn't a road going right to it. They didn't mind that she came here alone. They trusted her to be safe.

Today, she was lucky; it had rained at the end of the school day, fierce and brief. Now, an inch of water trickled through the usually dry bed that traveled through the cave. She crouched down, charting the way the creek expanded and changed. The dirt and debris that collected in the bed had already washed away. Now, clear, amber-hued water rippled on its journey. Somewhere, a spadefoot toad called for its mate. Sara stood and made her way forward, stepping as carefully as she could, trying not to splash, not to disturb anything that may have come.

The front area of the cave was...well, cavernous. Like a hall where Tolkien's dwarves might feast. It had taken Sara all summer to map it. There were ten wooden steps at the entrance, leftover from a time when some entrepreneur hoped for money and tourists. Then a small landing, where she'd sometimes find animal bones. (Never pellets, though. Whatever was eating the mice and voles and shrews, it wasn't an owl.) Pretty soon after, the sunlight reached its limit. The bats lived here. Sara sensed their small bodies overhead; the murmuring, the breathing, the rustling of a thousand leathery wings wrapped around one another.

Three tunnels led off from the main cavern. One dead-ended shortly after it began, a pile of rocks and debris. The tunnel walls were intact—no cave-in. And there were sandstone boulders mixed in amongst the basalt. Someone or something had moved them there.

The second tunnel wound its way for about half a mile before coming to a natural end.

The third tunnel. This was the one the stream traveled down, after a rain. This tunnel was wide, tall, echoing. It went on forever. Or at least seemed to. She was determined to reach the end, map it all.

There was something she hadn't added to the map yet, something she sensed but couldn't yet verify. It had been four weeks since she'd last heard it, something deep and primal, a reverberation that traveled up the basalt into her bones. When it reached the ossicles in her ears, she could sometimes make out words. *Be patient. Be brave.*

That was alright. Part of Sara's strength lay in her patience. She was cautious and respectful of everything she discovered, taking her time to study and learn. No one else saw these things. No one else noticed. Why would anything reveal itself to someone who didn't care?

Sun, rain, or snow, the school expelled students outside on their lunch breaks, to the playground and patchy lawn behind the building. Sara spent her breaks alone on the grass. She hated playgrounds. Asphalt forgave nothing; it ate knees and ankles. The forest liked when she ran and jumped and explored. It cushioned when she fell.

It was early October, still warm and comfortable in the sun. She sat on the lawn, absorbed in a small paperback with a taped-on cover. No matter how many times she read it, this scene was one of her favorites, where the princess confronted the dragon. She was so engrossed she didn't notice the shadow until it darkened the words on the page. Her head snapped up. Peter Harp loomed over her, his two best friends from lacrosse flanking his sides.

"Reading on break? You're a bigger nerd than I thought."

Every muscle in Sara's body coiled up tight. "What are you doing out here? You're second lunch."

"Didn't feel like English today. Guess I could do some reading, though." Before she could react, Peter grabbed her book. She felt the slice of a paper cut as she tried and failed to hold on. He showed the cover to his friends as she scrambled up.

"*Dealing with Dragons*?" He laughed too loud, for show. "She's reading a kids' book!"

"It's not a kids' book." She felt blood rushing to her cheeks. "You'd know that if you could read beyond a first-grade level."

Peter's face darkened. He threw the book back at her. It bounced off her arm and landed in the grass, spine splayed.

"You're writing my semester science report," he said.

She stood tall, squared her shoulders. Her voice shook. "I'm not doing your homework this year."

"Yeah, you are. Unless you want to spend every lunch with your face in the dirt."

"You can't beat up a girl."

He held up a hand, feigned offense. "I'm a feminist, Sara. I treat everyone equal." With another peal of laughter and a nod to his friends, they marched off.

Sara picked up the book, careful not to get blood from her cut on it. She stared at the familiar words she loved so much, but they blurred and refused to focus. Screw Peter Harp. This year was different. This year, someone understood.

"Can I show you something?"

Sunlight filtered through the pine trees and highlighted the too-long hair partially covering Roland's eyes. Sara reached into her bag, pulled out her social-studies book. "There's a cave I've been mapping. I think it's home to…something big."

She opened to the Oregon trail section, where she had a rough sketch of the main cavern. She pointed out the creek bed, the tunnel entrances, the nooks and crannies shaped by stalagmites.

Roland looked closely, flicking the hair out of his eyes. "You do all this in class?"

She grinned. "The teachers don't like it much."

He laughed. It always surprised her, how much she liked making him laugh. Roland turned the page to a sketch of the third tunnel, which dead-ended when it reached the edge of the page. "Is this all of it?"

"No. These are just my notes. I have more in my mapbook."

"Mapbook?" He looked up. "Can I see it?"

Sweat tickled her palms. This wasn't the direction she'd wanted the conversation to go. She wasn't ready to share that much yet. "That one stays home, to keep it safe."

To her relief, he shrugged and turned his attention back to the sketches. "Why do you think something lives here?"

She paused. *Be brave.* "I've noticed some signs of habitation. But I also can just *feel* it. I know something's there. And if I'm patient, I'll prove I'm worthy. It'll show itself to me."

Roland's face remained serious. She was sure her heart would bruise from the way it pounded against her sternum. "You don't believe me, do you?"

He looked up again, eyes wide. "Course I do. Friends believe each other, right?"

Her heart escaped her ribcage altogether and fluttered out on a long, slow exhale. She passed it off as a laugh, turned the page, and showed him more.

After two more times being 'caught' drawing in class, it was decided Sara should see the school counselor. 'Decided' by people other than Sara. No one seemed to care about her opinion on the matter.

"It's nothing to be ashamed of," her dad said. "We know you're fine."

"Middle school is an adjustment for a *lot* of people," added her mom.

If it was nothing to be ashamed of, why did the teacher sneak up to her in class, tell her in hushed tones it was time for her 'appointment'?

The counselor's office was a glorified broom closet. Miss Reyes smiled as Sara entered, said something about taking a seat. The wooden chair groaned as Sara sat, its old varnish warm under her hands. A fan under the desk pushed stale air around, its mechanical hum reminding her of conehead crickets in summer.

"I hear you've started off the school year on the wrong foot, Sara."

Sara pressed her fingers into the tacky varnish, unpeeled them slowly. "I wouldn't say that."

"Tell me a bit about yourself. Your parents..." Miss Reyes opened a file on her desk. "I don't know if I've seen them around school much."

"They're busy. They both have fellowships at the university."

"Academics!" Miss Reyes laughed. "You'd think they'd take more interest in their daughter's schooling."

"My mom says school isn't a good marker of intelligence."

Miss Reyes raised an eyebrow. "Interesting point of view. A few teachers mentioned you draw in class. What is it you draw?"

Now the backs of her thighs were sticking to the chair. "Just doodles."

"Well, they must be important. Mr. Hubert said you yelled at him when he took your notes away."

Sara remembered that day. Stupid Mr. Hubert had kept her notebook for two days, putting her behind on the tunnel. "It was *my* map. He had no right to take it."

Miss Reyes raised an eyebrow. "Well, you were working on it in class, Sara. But I understand that frustration. So you like maps, huh? I have a cousin who works for Google."

She wrinkled up her nose. "So?"

"Well, I know they aren't the only mapping technology out there, but—"

"Ugh, *no*." She couldn't help herself. She *hated* when adults assumed they knew. "That's not what I do. I draw fantastic maps."

"Oh!" Miss Reyes blinked. "You mean Narnia, that sort of thing?"

Sara rolled her eyes. "Not *fantasy* maps. *Fantastic* maps."

Again with that counselor smile. "I'm sure they are fantastic, you practice a lot."

She couldn't squash down her frustration any longer. "No, you don't get it." She unzipped her bag, pulled out her science book. "When people think of maps, they think of roads, rivers, mountains...that type of thing. But that's boring. Anybody can see that. You don't need a map for it. I make maps to what you *can't* see."

Miss Reyes studied the book. "What is this marked here?"

Sara looked where Miss Reyes was pointing. "Oh...well, these are just my quick notes...my real maps are back home. That's probably why you can't tell. It's a troll den."

Miss Reyes looked up. "This is very creative, Sara. But you do know it's not real, right?"

"I understand most people think that," Sara said. "My maps help them think differently."

"Sara...there's thinking differently, and then there's refusing to see reality. There are billions of people on earth—"

"Over seven billion."

Miss Reyes' smile grew a little tighter. "Exactly. So don't you think that if these things existed, someone would have seen them? Reported them?"

"Not if they're hiding. When a creature's environment shrinks, they shrink with it. Everyone thought Omura's whale was extinct. Then they found a whole group of them."

"That's the depths of the ocean, Sara."

"So? There are depths of the earth, too."

Miss Reyes folded her hands in front of her. "I think it's *wonderful* how imaginative you are. But don't you think you're getting too old for make-believe?"

"It's *not* make-believe," Sara said. "There are dragon stories from all over the world! England, China, Greece, India... they differ in appearance, but they're all obviously describing the same species."

"Sara..."

"And really, the variations make sense, that's normal with any type of animal across so many environments."

"Sara."

"I've been tracking data." She pulled out another book and flipped to a page in the middle. Its text was barely visible under a complex drawing of a tunnel system. "And it confirms what I've been thinking. These caves are the perfect environment for—"

"*Sara!*"

The raised voice startled her. She looked up from her sketches at Miss Reyes, whose palms were now flat on the desk. The counselor took a deep breath. "I think we're going to need more sessions than I originally thought."

A knock at the door—the shave-and-a-haircut rhythm that indicated her dad.

"How was school, Sar-bear?"

She sat on the bed, holding her mapbook. She didn't look over at him. "I don't know why you make me go there."

He sighed and sat next to her. "Didn't go well with the counselor?"

"She's awful, Dad. She tricked me into showing her my maps."

"I'm not sure 'tricked' is the—"

"She's so fake. I don't think she did one real thing the whole time I was there. And then when I showed her...she *wanted* to see them, and I showed her, and she just got mad."

He considered this. "I haven't seen your maps in a while. May I?"

Sara paused, then handed him the mapbook. He studied each page. "These are getting quite good. That's the glen to the east of the house, isn't it?"

Sara nodded.

"And this is..." he paused. "Actually, I'm not sure where this is."

"Tunnel three, in the cave. I'm not done with that one."

"Ah...don't mention this one to your mom, alright? She's not crazy about you exploring down there."

Sara kept her gaze on the page. "Dad, do you think my maps are stupid?"

"Well now. Let's think about that." He held the book out in front of them both. "These obviously require quite a bit of technical skill, which I can see is improving. They also require math to indicate elevation, grade change, and distance. Plus, you use logic to decide what's important to include. None of that sounds stupid to me."

Sara looked down at her feet. "Miss Reyes says none of it's real."

"Well...maps can do different things, you know."

She side-eyed him. "I *know*, Dad."

"Hear me out. Your maps...they may not be traditional, but I think they give you directions for paying attention. And that's very important. That's what scientists do every day." He handed her back the book. "But it's good to pay attention to what's in front of you, too. The real world can be scary. I know. But it creates a lot of amazing things, too."

She heard the word—*real*—and felt something inside her drop. "Ok, Dad."

He stood to leave and kissed her on the forehead. "That's my brave Sar-bear."

The deciduous trees turned umber and orange. Soon it would be too cold to sit together under the ponderosas' arms. But it was a dry fall, and today the sun shone. Sara's shoes were off. She stretched out her toes and dug them into the needles. Roland lay across from her, studying her latest drawings. Sara wiped Cheez-It dust off her fingers and flipped the page of his copy of *Maus*. She hoped he didn't notice how slowly she was reading. That she kept glancing over at him, trying to catch his reactions to her work. He really did remind her of a crow, the way he inspected and observed. Every once in a while his lips twitched up into a small smile, and she'd have to hide her own matching grin.

She was working up the nerve to ask him what he thought when his backpack buzzed. He turned off the alarm on his phone and started packing up. "I have to go. You can borrow that book tonight, if you want."

She tried not to look disappointed. "Where are you going?"

"Pegasus Pizza, with some guys from lacrosse."

What was this feeling inside her? Something afraid, something jealous. "Which guys?"

"Justin Rucinsky, Peter Harp, a few others."

She scowled. "Peter Harp's the worst."

"He's kind of annoying, but he's on the team." He stood, dusted pine needles off the back of his jeans.

"You don't *have* to go, you know," she said.

"Yeah, I do. My brother keeps bugging me, saying they're the 'cool kids' and I should hang out with them. This is the only way to get him to shut up." He shrugged. "See you tomorrow?"

She nodded and watched him walk away. Should she call after him, say something funny? Or should she look absorbed in her book, in case he looked back? She didn't know these things, couldn't figure out how to measure and draft them.

She pulled over her science book, still open to the page Roland had been looking at. A dragon crawled down the left margin. She didn't know these things, but maybe it didn't matter. Roland saw her—even the parts she did her best to hide—and he didn't look away.

The summer after Sara had turned six, her parents packed up the car and drove to another world. Or so it had seemed. Sara fell asleep in forest and woke up in a red land, with bridges and towers carved from sandstone.

"It looks like Spaceman Spiff," she said.

"Or maybe Spaceman Spiff looks like it," her mom said. "After all, Arches was here first."

Her dad had laughed. "Anything you can imagine, the earth churned up at some point."

Those words glued themselves into Sara's brain. *Anything you can imagine...* When they returned home, Sara pulled up Google Earth, panned around, zoomed in.

Here was a well that sucked up the sea into the earth. There, a pink lake surrounded by lush green jungle. Across the world, giant stepping stones led into the sea.

She never could have imagined all these things, yet there they were, each more fantastic than the next. The world made them. Maybe people didn't have the ability to dream up anything new. Maybe it was all there, hiding, waiting to be discovered.

"Are you ever scared?"

They sat under the pines, flipping through comics. Sara looked up. "When?"

"When you go into the cave. Isn't it dark?"

"Well, yeah. It *is* a cave." She smiled. "I have a headlamp and flashlight."

"Still..." Roland trailed off. "You don't know what's in there, right?"

"Not yet. But I will."

He paused, and Sara sensed he was gearing up for something. "Would you ever... I mean, could I come sometime?"

Anxiety settled in the bottom of her stomach. She reached out to touch the earth, grounded herself with long, stiff needles. "Well…you need special equipment."

"My mom has a flashlight in the emergency kit."

"And warm clothes and good shoes—it's really cold in there."

"That's easy."

"And a lot of other stuff, too," she added. "Stuff that's kind of hard to get."

"Well, I'll just stick next to you and we'll be fine."

Sara pictured the two of them together, her flashlight beam lifting up to reveal the huddled bats. The cold, clear air of the cave. Her exhale meeting his, mingling before disappearing together into the dark. She thought of the sounds, the shifting shadows, the near silence of the third tunnel as it wound its way through the earth. Of another pair of eyes seeing these things, recording, judging her place.

"Your mom probably wouldn't like it," she said.

"Why not? Your parents let you go."

"My parents are weird."

"So I won't tell my mom. She'll just think we're hanging out. Which would be true anyway."

His grin made her heart sink. She thought about saying yes—wanted to, she realized with surprise—but the voice still hadn't returned. She didn't know the rules, didn't know if it had to be only her, if it mattered if anyone else came…but she couldn't risk it.

"I just don't think it's a good idea, Roland."

His serious face darkened into something unfamiliar. "Why? You think I'm scared or something?"

"It's not that."

"So you're the *only one* allowed in there?"

"I didn't say that. It's just…" The thought of sharing the cave with someone else—*her* cave, the only space that truly knew—filled her with unnamed dread.

"Fine." Sara jerked back as Roland snatched the comic from under her nose and stood.

"What are you doing?" she said.

"I thought we were friends. But I guess not."

"No, Roland—"

"You know everyone talks about how weird you are, right? I didn't listen." He shrugged his backpack onto his shoulder—how well she knew that movement, the upward twitch of muscles—and stalked off.

The next morning, Roland wasn't waiting to walk to school. In math class, Sara wrote him a note.

Where were you?

She watched the folded piece of paper move slowly forward, two desks up and one to the right. Roland's hand reached out, the muscles on his slim shoulders moving as he unfolded it. Sara waited an eternity for it to make its way back.

Took the bus.

Sara blinked at the words, trying to figure out their meaning. She wrote back.

Are you mad at me

It took longer for the note to come return this time.

Yes.

Sara raised her pencil, trying not to panic, when the shadow loomed over her desk.

"Passing notes in class?"

She looked up, saw Mr. Hubert's frown. She heard necks swivel in her direction. She saw Roland, turned away, the only one in the class not staring.

"Do you understand why Mr. Hubert would be upset you were passing notes? It's very disrespectful, Sara."

Sara's fingers curled around the edge of her chair. Miss Reyes' office was cooler now, the varnish no longer tacky. In a few months the room would grow cold, a space heater under the desk instead of a fan.

"Who were you passing notes with?"

"No one."

Miss Reyes leaned forward. "Was it an imaginary friend?"

Sara shot over a glare. "I have real friends." A pain shot through her chest. Then, quietly: "He's mad at me."

"Ah." Miss Reyes' face softened. "It's normal for friends to fight, Sara. Conflict is part of any relationship. The important thing is how it's resolved. Saying 'sorry' can be hard, but it's important."

"But I didn't do anything wrong."

Miss Reyes leaned in closer, and for a moment Sara worried she'd take her hand. "Sorry never hurts, Sara. If the words feel too hard to say, a gesture can help, too."

The words were always hard to say. That was the good thing about the cave, the pines, the sky. The rocks and the water and wind. They communicated in a different way, a patient way. The earth never expected words. It accepted her as she was.

And, she realized, so did Roland.

After school, she sat in the entrance of the third tunnel, watched her breath condense and evaporate. She listened. Somewhere, the dripping of water. Her own chest rising and falling. She closed her eyes, willed whatever it was to return, to prove it had been real, to prove she wasn't...

The quiet pressed down, thick enough to feel, real enough to get lost in.

She opened her eyes. This *was* real, these sensations, these feelings, what lived and breathed beyond the casual eye. Of course they didn't want to be seen. Who would want to be exposed to such a careless world?

Roland wasn't careless, though. Roland was her friend.

Back home, she pulled out the mapbook, looked through the pages. She hadn't shown Roland she cared. But she could.

The next day, Sara walked to school alone, backpack heavy on her shoulders. It was a little too cold now for just her anorak. She walked quickly, in theory to stay warm, in reality to speed the morning along. She did her best to focus in class. She resisted the smell of lead, the empty margins. She couldn't get in trouble before lunch. She stole glances out the window, watched clouds swirl and gather.

First-lunch came. Sara ate in her regular spot on the lawn. It was warmer than it had been this morning, but the air was thick and heavy with the promise of rain, the first in weeks. She looked up at the dark clouds that blanketed the sky.

The bell rang, announcing the five-minute break between periods. The sounds of the schoolyard increased in a final release of energy as students went back inside. Sara tried to finish her food, but her stomach swirled as much as the clouds. Finally, the second bell rang.

Now she heard the wind moving through the sky, the small birds warning each other of the coming storm. She put out a hand, ran her fingers through the grass, noted each blade.

Then the rush came. She heard it growing, echoing in the halls, before it burst out into the open air. Second lunch. Sara stood, grabbed her bulky backpack, and walked around to the front of the building.

Even with his back toward her, she recognized him immediately. The slight slouch, the way he shuffled his feet. He stood in a group to the side of the basketball court.

Sara walked up and tapped him on the shoulder. Roland turned. She watched his eyes widen, his brows rise.

"What are you doing here? You have first lunch."

"I know. I have something to show you."

"What is *she* doing here?"

Her head snapped to the right. She'd been so intent on Roland she hadn't noticed the people he stood with: lacrosse players, including Peter Harp. He crossed his arms over his chest. "Finish my report?"

She swallowed and squared her shoulders. *Be brave.* "Could you come with me?" she said to Roland.

"You shouldn't be out here," he said. "You'll get in trouble."

"Hey, I asked you a question," Peter said. "Anybody home in there?" He was loud, using his 'look at me' voice. His cohort snickered. Roland didn't, though. Sara focused on him.

"It'll just take a minute."

"Just drop it, ok?" She saw his gaze dart around, track the gathering crowd. "I know your parents are ok with you getting in trouble, but my mom isn't."

"You won't get in trouble, I just…" But he was turning away. Desperate, watching her plan rapidly unravel, Sara unzipped her backpack, held it out in front of her. "I brought something to show you, it's really important and—"

Without warning, her backpack swung violently to the side, pulling her with it. Her arms shot out to steady herself, and it was only then she noticed Peter, his hand still extended from swatting the bag. She watched it fly out of her hands. She watched its entire contents scatter, notebooks, pens, markers, empty bags of Cheez-Its. Her mapbook flew out last, its beautiful silk cover skidding across the asphalt before landing right at Peter's feet.

She dove, too late. Her palms hit tar as Peter picked up the book.

"What's this..." His eyes widened as he studied the page in front of him.

Sara scrambled up, ignoring the sting in her palms and knees. "Give it back."

But he was laughing now, pointing at the book, playing it up for the crowd. "Oh my God. Do you see this? 'Signs of past dragon habitation. Witch's lair. Fairy glen.' She actually *is* crazy!"

There was more laughter now, rising on the wind, swirling around her. It hit Sara's ears one peal at a time, reverberating, traveling down her spine to tighten around her lungs, her heart. She looked at the faces, all staring at the mapbook as Peter turned the pages dramatically. She watched his mouth move as he sounded out the names, the locations, the discoveries. A ringmaster showing off the freakshow.

Sara sought the one face she wanted to see. Roland stood slightly behind Peter, his serious face staring at the mapbook. His gaze darted up, crow-like, and caught hers. Peter elbowed him in the side, and Roland's eyes flitted back to the page. Peter was pointing at something, waiting for a reaction. Roland paused just a second—a second that held worlds, that stretched to contain heartbeats—before his mouth turned up at the corners and he laughed.

She snatched the book from Peter's hands and shoved him, hard. By the time he hit the ground, she had already shouldered past the people behind her. She pushed past all the blurry faces and ran.

Asphalt turned to concrete turned to pine needles. Sara clutched the mapbook to her chest as she ran, felt its pressure against her. The rain started when she reached their meeting spot under the pines. Only a few drops, hitting her cheeks and running down to her lips.

Thunder clapped as she passed through the invisible curtain, the sheet that divided one world from the next. She ran down the ten steps, past the landing, into the main hall. She didn't pause to hear the bats, to see what new bones lay undisturbed. She ran, footsteps splashing through the rising creek. Her feet knew this place. They needed no light, no thought to guide them.

Sara's ragged breath echoed in her ears, off the walls. Everything, she wanted to wipe away everything: the laughter, the jeers, the shoulder shrug away. The notes passed, the sunny afternoons spent trading books, the walks to school. The tack of varnish on her fingertips, the teachers' frowns, the stupid, lonely patch of grass where she sat, alone, every lunch. The weight of the word: *real.* What was real? Sara's feet hitting stone, salt on her lips, her breath...

She stopped and stood still, tried to calm her beating chest. What had stopped her? A sense, a sound? She couldn't tell, not with her stupid heart filling her ears.

Be brave, Sara. Breathe in. Breathe out.

That was it—nothing. No steam as she exhaled, no condensation as the hot air from her body hit the cold air of the cave. She touched her arm. Her bare skin was warm.

She looked around—or tried to. When she put them in charge, her feet knew the way. Now...her eyes tried to adjust to the pitch black. She could hear a trickle of water at her feet. Was she in the third tunnel? She mentally retraced her steps. Had she come this far before? She drew in the hot air, realized it stank of rotten eggs. She began to gag, to panic, when she felt it traveling up her bones. *Close your eyes.*

She brushed her fingertips against stone, warm to the touch. The water had stopped; all she could hear were the sounds of her own body. Nothing else this far in the earth. Except...

Her eyes flew open and she held the mapbook closer to her chest. Her protection, her knowledge. Her proof that she knew this place, that it knew her. That she belonged.

She was sure she heard something now. Something beyond her echoing heart and careful steps and invisible breath. She recognized it from the bats: the scrape of leather wing on stone.

Sara peered into the dark. "Hello?"

There was a flare of light, small as a match, but in this inky blackness it made her squint. Still, she caught the shimmer of scale, the flicker of a long, forked tongue. She sensed rather than saw the vastness in front of her, the endlessness beyond the edge, everything, everywhere, waiting to be discovered.

An exhale answered: *Well done.*

See L.D. Oxford's story "The Girl Who Drew the World" online at Metaphorosis.
If you liked it, leave a comment. Authors love that!
Remember to subscribe to our e-mail updates so you'll know when new stories are posted.

About the story

I remember the exact moment when the seed of this story implanted in my brain. My husband and I were driving through western Montana on the way home from backpacking in Glacier National Park. Glacier is a primordial place; you can literally see the titanic forces that shaped the earth. I looked out the passenger window in awed reverence at this ancient, new-to-me land. It was morning, and we were in a mind-bogglingly green valley framed by metamorphic rock formations. The sun made them glow in a way that seemed other-worldly. And yet, amazingly, they were not other-worldly—they were right here, on this beautiful gem of an earth we get to live on.

From there, my brain went down some rabbit-holes. Could humans ever actually imagine something new? Or was it all inspired by the world around us? And if that were true...what about dragons? What about mermaids and puca and all the other things people have "made up"?

Sara and her story took shape from there. I wrote the entire first draft by hand, in dribs and drabs over the span of a few months. Six years and countless revisions later, "The Girl Who Drew the World" definitely counts as the most challenging story I've written. And I'd do it all again in a heartbeat.

A question for the author

Q: Do you often include children in your stories? What role do they play?

A: I do, both as side characters and in starring roles. Kids see the world in an entirely different way than adults. They haven't learned how things are "supposed" to work yet. What we view as mundane is wondrous to them—and things an adult would find unbelievable can be "normal" to a kid. Writing a story from a child's point of view opens up entirely new possibilities, especially in speculative fiction.

About the author

L.D. Oxford writes speculative fiction and recently completed her first novel. When she's not writing or working a day job, you can find her playing with paint, digging in dirt, or satisfying her travel bug. She lives with her family in Seattle.

@ld_oxford

The Heebie-Jeebie Beam

E.C. Fuller

I thought I found a toy raygun. It looked like a toy, at least. I'd been rummaging around in Dad's backyard workshop for props when I found it in a dusty black briefcase wedged between an old laptop and a beige filing cabinet. Chisel-like marks cut into the scuffed leather and busted brass latches, as if someone had broken into it. Nestled in emerald velvet, the raygun's body was orange and blue-painted metal and was shaped more like a glue-gun than a Glock. It also had a marble-sized glass ball plugging the hole where the ray would come out. On the side of the gun was a dial that went from

0 to 5. *Bingo-bango*, I thought. *This is exactly what I need.* And I should have remembered then that I was never a good thinker.

Despite that, I couldn't help thinking anyway. It was weird that the workshop hadn't been locked. Everything inside it had a mother's-worth of warnings: *watch fingers, sharp objects, do not use while intoxicated, may cause dizziness.* Dad had rarely let me past the tiny welcome mat, and never alone. But he was gone and I was curious and in need of cool shit for the play. I hoped he'd left the raygun for me, though I couldn't imagine him doing that.

Before I left the workshop, I tested the door to the glass and metal cabinet. Behind the glass were machines that looked like football helmets crossed with MRI machines. Dad had explained what they did after a salvo of begging, a slight smile on his normally unsmiling face.

Each helmet had a warning on a business-card-sized placard with a number in the 700s. The 700s meant that the invention was in "the series of inventions that alter consciousness through emotional stimulation," he'd told me. 712 made you believe you were an empty suit of clothes. 722 made you feel like someone was watching you. 738 made you feel like you were watching everyone, your sight divided like a dragonfly's.

"These aren't dangerous," I had said to Dad, disappointed.

He had replied, "Altered states of being are the most deadly things of all." A very Dad-ly thing to say. I remember being impressed by his high-falutin' words, though I didn't understand what he meant at the time, nor did I really believe him. It's hard to take souped-up helmets seriously. Ditto for a raygun. Yet, the number 743 was etched into a brass plate on its briefcase's cover: the highest number I'd ever seen. He had taken the higher numbers in the 700 series with him. The other series, he had dismantled or melted down.

I left the dusty workshop, turning the raygun in my hands, and looked round the backyard for something to test it on. The raygun must have been one of the last inventions Dad made when he was here. He'd made hundreds, and not a single one was made as a joke, or art, or decoration. Each one did *something*. But how did I safely find out what the raygun's something was?

The backyard was a square of yellow, brittle grass hemmed by a high wooden fence. The fence had targets painted on the slats, asterisked with scorch marks. Where Dad had poured his chemicals was bald dirt in which grass would never green again. A brave, gnarled redbud tree by the workshop had been left alone. Under its scant shade, my friend Michael chanted his lines. "Elementary, dear Wallace. Not Middle School. Elementary School." Dad'd built robots that could emote better than Michael. But he was still my best bud and I didn't want to test an unknown invention on him unless I absolutely had to.

While Michael gestured at an invisible audience, I clicked the dial to one and aimed at one of the targets on the fence. When I pulled the trigger, a green beam of light fell on the target like a flashlight. No sound. Nothing happened. A perfectly cromulent outcome for an invention that affects the brain. But it's best to first test gun-shaped things on things that don't bleed.

But all things that bleed have brains. Now, I needed a new target. A squirrel flicked its tail near the wooden fence. I beamed the squirrel. It froze. When I released the trigger, the squirrel bolted up the redbud and scampered to the roof.

The squirrel zooming past Michael's ankle made him yelp and jerk his leg to his chest.

"Perfect," I said. "Do that when the corpse is revealed."

"Willie, what the fudge are you doing?" he asked indignantly.

"Testing something." I held up the raygun. The squirrel had not died or acted in non-squirrely ways, which was a positive sign. It was possible that the effect took a while to work. But none of Dad's inventions were zap-and-done deals. The 712 helmet, for example, required at least an hour of wearing before the user tried to fold themselves into a drawer. I just needed to know enough to make a good guess. "Go stand in front of the tree. I need to know what this does."

"Aw, I don't want to be nobody's lab rat. Especially not your Dad's. Why me and not you?"

" 'Cause your family has better health insurance than mine."

"I don't want to be no lab rat," he repeated. "You know how I feel about animal research."

"Then I'm out of the running, dude." He sniggered. But I wasn't done. "Listen: Dad invents stuff for medical research. His stuff is saving lives around the world *right now*. If you don't want a guinea pig to be a guinea pig, you gotta be one yourself."

He considered this. Then he positioned himself in front of the trunk. He stuck out his hips and pointed at me in a dramatic pose. I beamed him.

When the green light hit him, he made a funny face. I released the trigger.

"That felt weird," he said. "Do it again."

His expression this time was near a scowl.

"I don't know what I'm feeling, man."

"Lemme go up a level." I dialed to level two and beamed him again. He shuddered. If his expression on level one had been like that of a pedestrian running into a stranger, his expression on level two was of that same pedestrian being told he had nice skin.

"One more," he said cautiously.

I dialed to three and hit him again.

"Woo!" Now his expression was that of the pedestrian returning home to find the stranger waiting for him with lotion and rope. "It gives you the heebie-jeebies! Let me try."

I handed it over and braced myself for the beam. But Michael shoved the gun under his chin and pulled the trigger. He paled and his skin pimpled. He held down the trigger so long that I said sharply, "Dude?"

"It feels good when you stop." He smiled goopily. "Try."

He beamed me. The level three setting made your brain feel like a pot of water over a blowtorch. My thoughts boiled. *Oh God, I should not have taken it out of its case. This is why Dad left. Because I touched all his stuff. He's watching through the cameras he left in his workshop, the mirrors Mom covers up, and the squirrel, and he knows I touched his stuff.*

Michael released the trigger. The relief washed over me, cool and sweet and soothing. "Daaaaaang."

"Why'd he make it?" Michael asked.

"I dunno."

We beamed each other back and forth until we agreed. The first level made you feel like something was off. Level two stirred your thoughts into an anxious simmer. Level three made the hair on the back of your neck rise. I eyed that squirrel watching us from the workshop roof. Who knew what insane thoughts churned behind his dewdrop eyes?

But the bigger question was: why had Dad made a gun that scared people? Trying to figure out what Dad was thinking had obsessed me since I knew what thinking was. This was a man who'd stay up late in his workshop with his hands running through his thinning brown hair over questions with more Latin than English, more numbers than letters, whose answers were more confusing than their question. Late enough that the sun had quit the sky and the yellow light from his window threw a bright square on the grass, and I'd fall asleep with my cheek against the night-chilled window. He'd beat me to breakfast, scratching out his thoughts on the dining room chalkboard. I'd ask him what he was working on, knowing that by the time he'd finish answering, the school bus would be grumbling past the house.

"School is important," he would mutter as he drove me to school. "I know you're curious about my work—it makes me happy that you want to follow in my footsteps. But you can't miss school, you understand? You need to learn everything you can."

I could not imagine Dad being so careless that he'd leave an invention behind by accident.

When Michael's mom dropped us off at the high school auditorium the following night, she caught me just before I got out of her van.

"Have you heard from your dad?" she asked in a deceptively casual voice.

I had prepared sassy retorts to stupid questions like, "Where's your dad?" or "How's your mom doing?" But Dad hadn't even responded to my own texts and voicemails, like, "Mom's not mad anymore", "Are you alive?", and "I'm sorry." I wanted to retort now, "No, he's busy researching ways to heal Mom." But I didn't know if he was doing that anymore. So I just said no.

Her nostrils flared. She had showed up on our porch a week after Dad left, holding a covered casserole dish.

I'd been standing behind Mom when she answered the door, so I only saw her stooped back, like a parenthesis missing its partner. Michael's mom's eyes drifted to the wreckage behind us: bloated trashbags of Dad's clothes, the big, crumbling hole in the wall where Mom had thrown a plate at his head, and the small crumbling holes dotting the walls where she had drilled for the listening devices she accused him of hiding. I imagined Michael's mother could pick up the remaining psychic vibrations from the last words Dad had said: "I can't take you people anymore!"

Michael's mom said, as we clambered out of the van, "You'll both steal everyone's hearts tonight."

Our play was called, "The Curious Case of T.B.D." It had started as a joke name as we brainstormed suitably funny names, but none tickled us as much as T.B.D. So we had the houndstooth cape, the deerstalker caps, the British accents and pipes, and now the gun. All we needed now was to fix Michael's tendency to freeze before groups larger than three people.

Michael stared at a point in space, pale and clammy. I would've encouraged him to take deep breaths, but backstage was as odoriferous as an armpit.

"You practiced real good," I said.

He didn't respond.

"Listen, we're not the best anyway. Nobody will remember us! So do your lines, we get our extra-credit from Mrs. Green, and we can go to Wendy's afterwards."

Nada. It was time to bestow upon him my secret technique.

"Imagine the audience naked," I said. "The energy keeping you afraid will flow to your boner. And nobody in the crowd will notice your lightswitch dick."

He peeled open his gnawed-bloody lips. "This is why your Dad doesn't fucking love you."

I felt like he had shot me. "You know what? You know what?" I said as I cranked the dial to four. I beamed him. Immediately I wished I hadn't. His skin grayed. His mouth gaped, and his pulse fluttered in his throat. When I released the trigger, he gasped, color flooding his cheeks.

"Dude?" I said after a beat. His gaze unfocused and relaxed. My heart galloped in my throat. Stupid, stupid, stupid. "You okay?"

Our names blared over the intercom.

"William and Michael, starring in 'The Curious Case of T.B.D.'" I was supposed to lead Michael on-stage, where my fat ass would shield him from the audience long enough for him to stammer his first lines: "Wot's all this then?"

He checked the audience through the curtain, not with the mortal calm of a man being led to his execution, but with bewilderment, as if he had been asked something he hadn't expected. Without waiting for me, he strode out to center stage. The spotlight set him ablaze, and he planted his hands on his hips, drank in the audience, and projected his voice, "So what the frick-frack-snaps happened here?" The audience roared, and a huge grin opened his face.

Michael pranced around the stage. He ad-libbed quips that seemed bespoke, as if a Hollywood writer's spirit had possessed him. He did a goddamn backflip! People rocked and screamed with laughter.

After the show, other students slapped his back and tousled his curly hair. In the stage wings, he glowed.

"Dude, the beam did something to me," he said. "It cured me!"

We'd both beamed each other multiple times before the play and nothing had happened. What did the level 4 setting do? Dad's voice echoed in my thoughts: *we need a larger sample size.*

I scanned the talent-show hopefuls left. There, just about to go onstage, was Jenna. She swallowed as she peeked through the curtain. Even in the wan light, she looked green.

I said, "Hey Jenna, would you like to contribute to science?"

She dropped the curtain. "Is your dad looking for test subjects? Didn't he get a warning from some medical group about not taking the right safety measures?"

"Those charges were unsubstantiated," I snapped. "I'm testing something. You just need to stand still."

"What does it do?"

"It might make you the best performer of all time."

Jenna, an honor student destined to be called Your Honor, who couldn't read a newspaper without a red pen, whom Dad would have loved to swap me for, narrowed her eyes. "Okay."

I beamed her. She dropped the tennis balls she was going to juggle. She wilted and whimpered. I felt awful seeing her eyes well up, but I knew it wouldn't hurt her. After five seconds, I released the trigger. She dragged herself upright. Wonder stole over her face, and bemusement. She snatched her balls and ran out on stage, where she murdered our murder mystery in skill, humor, and balls.

To any student who looked nauseous, I cajoled, "You sir! Do you want to be a star? Young lady! Care to turn your stage fright into stage love?" In total, five students, plus Michael, went on stage like they were born for it. Their stage fright vanished the moment applause crashed over them.

Except Nancy. Seeing the formerly weak-kneed and spotlight-shy transform, she demanded to be beamed. I obliged her. But when her eyes rolled back in her head, the front of her jean skirt darkened. I stopped beaming her at once. Before I could apologize or offer my hoodie to tie around her waist, she fled the wings, sobbing. Oops.

Why hadn't it worked on her? I needed to know for myself. Before we went back onstage for the winner's announcement, I told Michael, "Beam me." He did.

Holy fuck.

Level 4 was like being an ant frying under a little boy's magnifying glass. And the little boy was me, telling me in the voice of Truth that I was destined to fail and be failed. That God had skipped me when he was supposed to put in something to love. That God's face was Dad's face, distant and cold like the moon. He had turned from me and he would never look back.

When the beam stopped, the sunlight of clarity flooded the canyons of my brain. It had all been my imagination. I floated out on stage to receive our Audience Favorite award, waved dreamily at the applauding audience, and puzzled languidly as Michael did another backflip to sonorous applause.

Following instructions from a Youtube video, I picked the lock on Dad's filing cabinet. I found folders fat with schematics, instructions, graphs, and notes. Each was labeled 0-100, 101-200, etc. The one for the raygun (which I named the Heebie-Jeebie Beam) had papers thick with gibberish: 'elevate cortisol', 'mild hypnosis', and 'transformative events'.

I snuck the file out of the workshop and spread my desk with my calculus homework in case Mom came in. I hid the Beam in its case behind my bookshelf. She checked on me every fifteen minutes through the crack in the door. Sometimes she stared wordlessly when I yelled at her to go away. I felt guilty for yelling. I used to yell at her all the time, especially when she started to refuse to leave the house. She'd developed a fear of computers, phones, and appliances, and unplugged them when she could. The manager at our local grocery store had banned her when she unplugged a freezer. So now I had to bike across town to the other grocery store. And I'd had to help her design and build an icebox that didn't use electricity, because we couldn't live without cold milk. It took weeks.

Now I couldn't stop thinking of the time her psychiatrist had caught me in the waiting room after one of her sessions and told me to be patient.

"She needs you right now," she had said. "You're the man of the house."

"But that's supposed to be Dad," I said. I had been thirteen then, and felt like I was wearing Dad's huge lab coat and drowning in it. The psychiatrist reminded me of a kindergarten teacher, all gentleness and cheer.

"He's not here right now. Somebody has to help her." *Obviously*, Dad would say. Dad had tried to fix Mom. They'd spend hours in his workshop. She'd come out all quiet and blank, and he would be tight-faced and brooding. When I asked if I could help, he said, "And what would that accomplish?"

"I'm not asking you to fix her," the psychiatrist had said, as if she could read my mind. "Sometimes things can be not our fault and still our responsibility. Her condition is not her fault, nor yours. Still, it's hers to manage. And she needs your help. You've already helped her, by telling your teacher what was happening at home."

When I had complained about my arms hurting from mixing adobe, digging trenches for molten ice, and trying to source goat hair, my teacher overheard and asked, "Son, are you building a yakhchāl?" I didn't want to tell him. It's embarrassing to have a crazy mom. People pity you. Then, they wonder if it's genetic. But the bags under my eyes, mud caked in my hands, and wealth of knowledge about ancient Persian architecture for refrigeration gave me and her away. That, and because I cried.

The psychiatrist had said, "I don't doubt that you need help too, William. You've already done oodles on your own.

More than many of the adults in the same situation as you. Right?" I shrugged-nodded-wiggled in embarrassment, mystified. "Once we find the combination of medication, therapy, and social support your mother needs, things will get much easier. Remember to be kind to her, and to yourself."

So I chewed my cheeks when my anger rose, and sometimes I could hold it in, and sometimes I couldn't. Strangely, she seemed to relax when I yelled. Her shoulders would lower from around her ears and her tightly held mouth would ease. That made me feel a billion times worse, and I couldn't figure out why.

Why don't you understand this, William? Dad's voice cut through my thoughts, rapping on my skull as his knuckles used to. *You can do it. You just aren't trying hard enough.* I was dangerously close to thinking, If you couldn't help her, I totally can't. But seeing how Michael and the other theater kids had transformed for the better, I thought instead that maybe the Heebie-Jeebie Beam could do the same for her. I had his notes, dictionary.com, and a new pack of colored highlighters. I might not have his big brain, but I could tickle the keyboard until the search engines gave me what I needed..

But he hadn't made understanding his notes easy. The instruction manual was crammed with sentences like this: "A transformative experience is marked by both a personal and epistemic metamorphosis following the experience."

And reading that smug middle-finger of a sentence, I thought, *Why didn't you just explain it to me in a way I could understand? Instead of leaving mysteries everywhere, or your family's future TBD?*

I skimmed. I translated paragraph by paragraph. I googled, googled, and googled, and wept some. A few days later I had hit the last page and found a note in his perfect loopy handwriting: *Invention 743 is a failure.*

The Heebie-Jeebie Beam turned out to be the perfect name. The Beam stimulated fear and anxiety in the recipient. Dad had built it as a nonviolent defense for the CIA. Scare a pursuer silly and skedaddle. But because he had been researching emotions, he thought he might use it to change people. An unexpected side effect of the Beam was a sort of artificial catharsis. The list of suggested changes included things like: *more reflective, more compassionate,* and *more respectful of the advancement of humankind and the demands caused by the pursuit thereof* (that last one was circled).

Dad hypothesized that strong emotion—like birth of your firstborn, death of your parents, ghost pepper-strength emotions—coupled with some kind of catalyst would snap people into turning their lives around. He thought the catalyst would be some sort of experience, but what kind, how long, where, and when?

Sucked that he'd never been able to figure out how to use the Heebie-Jeebie Beam to get people to change. He'd tested short and long term results on subject 'M' without success, though the page detailing the results was ripped out.

Bupkiss, he wrote.

Had Michael and I accidentally discovered how to make the Beam work? The five kids with stage fright who'd been beamed joined the theater club, cheer, and formed bands. Maybe that was why the Beam hadn't worked on me. I didn't have stage fright to begin with, so there was nothing to transform.

But there was the fifth level, just a click of the dial away.

I didn't have time to read deeper than the methodologies section of his notes. Mom demanded I help her sweep the house for recording devices, and I had to hide all my notes. We rummaged in the back of the cabinets. We parted each leaf of our house plants. We took down pictures on the wall, checked inside their frames, and rehung them. The family we had been in those pictures was looking weary of her antics.

I played with the idea of telling Mom I'd found an invention. But lately she wouldn't even respond to what I said. She'd stare at me from across at the dinner table as I shoveled casserole into my mouth and until I escaped to my bedroom. Sometimes I caught her checking dishes I'd just put away, or peeking under folds of laundry.

As I did dishes, I wondered how to get her to be normal again. I used to imagine her at her power plant job standing in front of dials, gauges, and control panels, pressing the buttons that told electricity to zap here or there. She'd won a mug for it. It said, World's Best Nuclear Power Plant Controller. I scrubbed it free of tea stains and put it on the shelf next to its mug friend, Meltdowns Are Only Good with Cheese. It wasn't her fault her brain didn't regulate its own chemicals right.

Could the Beam work on her? She was definitely scared of something. But then I imagined how it felt to get beamed at level 5, and the hair rose on my arms. I couldn't do that to her. I felt sick for thinking it. But I couldn't imagine that the lower levels would be strong enough to cure what ailed her.

I got why Dad had left her. I just didn't get why he'd left me. I kept thinking about how Dad had said, "I can't stand you *people*." I was in that *people*. What if the Beam had been meant for me? To wrinkle my smooth brain like a reverse iron, and make me into the son he wanted?

"Will?" Mom asked. "What's wrong?"

"Nothing," I lied. "I have a project. Scary stuff, big part of my grade. I'm going to Michael's."

It was easier to run away to somewhere where a mom or dad could shoot me finger-guns and ask, "What can I do yah for, my dude?" And dream of the day where I could say "Nothing," and mean it. I was afraid he would never come back, and that day would never come.

A few days later, I came home from school to a bonfire roaring in the backyard. It chewed on bookshelves, made charred lace out of documents. Mom carried an armful of old notebooks out of the workshop and dumped them in the fire. The pages shriveled; a diagram of the human brain blackened. Her fly-aways smoked. She panted, wide-eyed.

I ran to the workshop. The shelves inside were bare, dust marking where books had lain or cabinets had stood. She'd swept all his chemistry glassware into a cardboard box by the side of the door. The pieces sparkled. The odor of chemicals stung my lungs.

I demanded in a high voice that didn't sound like mine, "What are you doing?"

Her face slacked. She began the staring I hated.

"Spring cleaning," she replied, scanning my face.

Stay frosty, I told myself. *What would Dad do?* Think. Dad would think.

"Let me keep his files," I said.

"Why do you need them?" she asked suspiciously.

"I— I want to read them."

"You don't read."

"I'm going to," I said honestly. "New Year's Resolution."

She stared at me. If she had been angry, scared, worried, or *something*, I could have talked her down. But her face was blank, as it was more and more these days.

My throat clenched. But I asked jokingly, "Why do you need to burn them?"

"Because I'm burning everything."

Then I saw the picture frames. I had mistaken them for branches. I had mistaken the charred dress shirts for part of our shadows, and the chair Dad liked to sit in as more branches. A weird roaring filled my ears.

Mom pointed inside. "Go get the rest of the pictures off the wall. I'll get the workshop."

"But—" I thought, if I got the workshop, Mom might find the Beam in my room. But if I didn't save the workshop, Dad might never come back.

Maybe there was a way I could save both.

I ran to my room. The hallways were patchy where pictures had blocked the sunlight from dulling the paint. My room hadn't been touched. I yanked the case from its hiding place and the instructions fanned upon the floor.

I dialed the Beam to level 5 and jammed it under my chin. There had been no scale or description for the levels in Dad's notes. I didn't even know exactly how it worked, except that it worked best when you were afraid. My heart raced as if trying to escape from the raygun in my hand. Negative effects? What could be worse than what was happening? Than what had been happening since Dad left? *Please work*, I thought. *Help me understand.*

I must have pressed the trigger. I don't remember. It was only after, when my hand fell and the Beam dropped in my lap, that I came to.

Level 5 showed me something that had already happened. Level 5 was a molasses dream, a slowed down vision, of Dad endlessly pushing the key into the house's lock for the last time. I'd been standing stupidly (the only way I stand) with tears and snot running down my dumb face, while Mom stormed off to her room. Level 5 showed me things I'd noticed, but not put together. That Dad had filled his car with gas, some notebooks, some inventions, some laundry he didn't bother to fold. On the table were the math workbooks he'd go over with me, me squirming and not getting it, him hawkish and sharpening with irritation. He pushed the key into the lock, like a dagger into the heart, knowing I was still inside.

Lifting Level 5 did not bring relief. It brought clarity. It emptied the nothing I had cottoning up my brain and replaced it with more nothing, so that I could remember what had really happened without my fear getting in the way.

The worst had happened when Dad had left. But the worst needed to happen to show us why him leaving was actually the best thing that could have happened.

I don't know how long I slumped there on the floor with the Beam in my lap, pondering this, coming down from the effect. The sound that brought me back to reality was Mom's footsteps coming close.

"William, what is taking so long?"

I had a hunch, but there was no time to test it. I no longer hoped Dad would come back, or that I would become smarter, but I was still afraid Mom would be lost. What the Beam did—what I *thought* the Beam did—I hoped would bring her to reality, the way it had for me.

She opened the door to my room to me pointing the Beam at her. I reasoned I'd only pull the trigger for five seconds. But her face, pulled long in horror and anguish, made my stomach quiver. She sagged against the door.

"I didn't pull the trigger!" I said. "I didn't!" I threw the Beam on my bed and held up my hands.

She drew herself up with visible effort and towered over me.

"I knew it! I knew he swapped you! How has he been talking to you, huh? Where did he plant them?"

"I—what?"

Her open palm cracked against my cheek. It was the first time she'd ever hit me.

"I didn't... He didn't..." I sobbed. Had the trigger been pulled somehow? Mom saw me glance at the Beam and dove for it.

She beamed me.

Like before, Level 5 showed me nothing new. But what it did show multiplied exponentially like a face in a broken mirror as she trained the seasick-green light on my head. Her white-rimmed eyes moist and red-veined, over the dinner table, across the hall, over the kitchen counter, through the windshield, and craning over me as I lay on the ground. The sun was one of her eyes, and the moon was another one. The eyes of squirrels were hers and so were Michael's. They winked in the reflections of the floorboards and shone in the holes of the wall siding as she dragged me out of the room. They winked in my brain as my head bounced down the steps and filled my vision as she tugged my leg, grunting, to the bonfire.

The social worker told me later that a neighbor saw her, tackled her, and threw me in his pool to put out the flames. He then had to fight Mom off when she attacked him with gardening shears, and then save me from drowning because I was still unconscious.

"I wanna be him when I grow up," I slurred from the hospital bed.

"Me too," the social worker agreed.

Mom told the police that her husband had kidnapped me and replaced me with a robot. I'd been acting strange since Dad left. Helping her clean. Doing homework. Reading. She didn't know for sure, until I pointed her husband's raygun at her. She said Dad had been using the Beam on her for a long time. She knew the real William would never point the gun at her. He would never pull the trigger. Her worst nightmare had come to life. But also, joy: it *wasn't* me. And she needed the police's help to find her husband and real son.

"I didn't pull the trigger," I sobbed. And a little voice inside me replied, *But you pointed the Beam.* I sure didn't look like William or Willie anymore. I looked like an action figure left on its side on a hotplate. When the doctor ordered some x-rays, in case I had worse injuries, I felt relieved that I had bones, not articulated plastic joints. Still, I asked Michael and his parents to call me Will.

In the following weeks I stayed with Michael and his parents and helped him start his band, Micycle Ride. He swung his microphone around on its cable, thrust his hips, and sang like he'd die without music, his glasses streaked with sweat and his smile ear to ear. Sometimes he'd surprise me into smiling too. In the notebook my therapist gave me, I wrote song lyrics, how I felt about it all, and what I thought happened. I also reread the instruction manual and research notes for the Beam, googled some more, and thought about how it worked. When I wrote my hypothesis in my notebook and felt its rightness like a tuning fork, I decided that I would never shoot anyone with the Beam again.

I guess Dad really did have us bugged, because his Volvo rolled into Michael's driveway about a week after I left the hospital. Michael's parents came to my bedroom doorway to tell me, like the very incarnations of motherly and fatherly concern.

Dad stood on the front steps. He looked shrunken, and the lines between his eyebrows had deepened. When he saw me, his eyebrows jumped. I had not gotten prettier since leaving the hospital.

I said nothing and waited.

"William," he said at last, awkwardly. "How are you?"

I raised the eyebrow I had left and didn't reply. His starch dissolved as he perspired before me. He dropped his gaze to the welcome mat.

"Well... come along," he said, gesturing to his car. I snorted. He had the gall to look startled. Emotions passed across his face. I didn't know what I wanted to say to him. I felt almost sorry for him. I almost wanted to apologize for snorting. But what I actually wanted was too numerous to list, too huge to name, and too painful to speak aloud. At last he looked at Michael's parents. They put their hands on my shoulders. I felt my heart overflow, even as he said to them, "I'll send a monthly stipend for William." And he turned to get back in his Volvo.

Fear clutched my heart, and that clutch was broken by rage. He could not get away scot-free. He would be the guinea pig this time.

"Hey," I said, my voice cracking. He paused with the key in his hand. "Did you ever use the Heebie-Jeebie Beam on yourself?"

"The what?"

"The raygun."

His eyebrows quirked. "The Fear Gun," he said in the voice of impending snark. "No. Why would I use it on myself?"

His tone harmonized with the past tones he had used when he asked questions, questions with unspoken contempt and judgment that crushed me small and made me believe I was smooth-brained, simple-minded. But since he had been gone, I had grown as tall as he was. At eye-level, I could truly see what I had always known. Dad had remained Dad, backwards and forwards. Mom's condition and mine hadn't changed him one bit. I felt then what he must have felt looking at me while my tears wet my calculus homework. It was so simple, what I needed him to understand. I threw back what he gave me in his own word: "Dumbass."

Dad's face whitened. It colored in patches as his eyebrows drew together and his mouth opened, but my ruined body denied his words, and he dropped his eyes. He raised a finger to shake it in my face, but then made a fist, made a strangled noise, and made an expansive gesture—at what? I didn't care.

When he left, I could see him with his knuckles raised to his mouth in his little dinged-up Volvo.

Watching him leave made me feel a curious lightness and nausea. The lightness left me undone, and I went upstairs to cry privately and write in my journal: *Dad's actions confirm my hypothesis about the Heebie Jeebie Beam.*

The Heebie Jeebie Beam worked, but not the way Dad thought it would. The Beam didn't work by stimulating fear. It stimulated the recipient's strongest belief.

Specifically, it manifested the worst-case scenario of that belief—being booed offstage, your husband and child being imposters, your hero abandoning you. The levels manifested the beliefs at different strengths, for those that need more neurochemical power to unroot. When paired with an experience that showed that what happened was different from how you believed it would go, the belief broke, and the recipient was altered. Not in the ways Dad thought they would be.

But that's the kicker. You have to face your fears. And you can't make someone do it if they don't want to. Worse, sometimes what you think people are afraid of isn't actually the thing they're afraid of. Frightening someone without showing them something that neutralizes that fear is just torture. You don't need the Beam to know this, or even cause someone to change, as my experiment on Dad confirmed. I hypothesized that Dad called me stupid and experimented on Mom because he himself felt stupid and broken. So when I called him a dumbass, his reaction proved it.

It was hard to write this hypothesis in my composition notebook. It meant that what happened to me and Mom wasn't what he was afraid of. I don't know what would change his ways, if what happened to us didn't.

The more I thought about the Beam, the more I marveled at it. Man, he hadn't known what he had. A tool that confronts you with what you believe? How many people live their lives not knowing what they believe? Or their deepest fear? What had he been thinking?

In the weeks and months following Dad showing up and dipping out, I got really into song-writing. I thought about writing non-fiction, investigating all the ways people do or don't change. But singing came easy to me, and I needed something easy in my life. Making bangers in the basement on an old synthesizer and howling out my feelings was good medicine. Anyway, I wrote some ditties about everything. When my burns are better, Michael and I are gonna try to get some gigs. Though, getting up on stage, getting gawked at, and then singing about my feelings? And what if we get famous, and Mom hears our jams? The thought of going on stage and fumbling my slippery heart gives me the willies.

Yet, one night, under the yellow light of the lamp, at the hour ruled by crickets and owls, I had been thinking about fear, and Mom, and Dad. Word by word, I wrote the final lines to a song I'd been waiting to hear.

Be afraid!
What are the Heebie Jeebies but knowing you've got something to lose?
Loving each other is how we'll survive
To fear is to know we're alive.

See E.C. Fuller's story "The Heebie-Jeebie Beam" online at Metaphorosis.
If you liked it, leave a comment. Authors love that!
Remember to subscribe to our e-mail updates so you'll know when new stories are posted.

About the story

When I wrote "The Heebie-Jeebie Beam", I had no expectations for the story. One of my New Year's Resolutions was to stop spending so much time on a single short story. It wasn't uncommon to spend tens of hours writing and rewriting one, so my main goal was to take a short story from concept to accepted publication in under 15 hours. I had been obsessed with the phrase, "the heebie-jeebies" and had been playing around with ideas that dealt with inventions. On top of this, I felt like I had been writing too many serious, heavy stories. I wanted to write something fun and not think too hard about the story.

However, when I got past the midpoint, I couldn't help but think more seriously about the Beam itself. What kind of person makes a raygun that frightens people? Why do we feel fear, and how far would we go to stop ourselves from feeling afraid? At the time of writing, I was also interested in the theory of aspiration, or the philosophy of trying to become a certain person (especially the book by Agnes Callard). That made its way into the story as well.

As I revised, the story became more personal. A member of my family had suffered flare ups of mental illness throughout my life, starting when I was in middle school and continuing through post-college. The worst period was a year-long episode where they did many of the things the mother in the story did — the staring, the checking of the appliances and photograph frames, and persistent, strange questioning were regular occurrences. I felt that much of the responsibility for getting them help fell on my shoulders. I tried to reason with them, keep their spirits up, drove them to the local psychiatric hospital — sometimes at midnight — resenting other family for checking out, loathing myself for wishing I could do so myself, wishing someone would come and "fix" things, and spending hours researching their illness or trying to be a gentler, kinder, more understanding person (which I failed to be over and over again). But you can't self-improve yourself into fixing someone else, and sometimes the only way out of a bad situation is to let it pass. Only time and a change of medication eased their condition.

A question for the author

Q: If you could talk to your novice-writer self, what bit of advice would you give?

A: There's a difference between being a writer and being a storyteller, and the faster you understand the difference, the happier you'll be with your own work. Better still if you understand the basic definition of a story: a story is about someone trying to do something difficult and how they change inwardly as a result. But don't abandon your love of stories of ideas, philosophies, or other abstract things, because — though it'll be more difficult to write about those things — those are what fulfill you and make your stories so unique. And more people will love them than you think!

And don't be afraid to change what/how you write if you think it means betraying yourself. If you change in order to better chase your dreams, then you become more you than if you changed nothing.

About the author

E.C. Fuller grew up in Claremore, Oklahoma and graduated from the University of Chicago in 2016. She is the short story category winner of the 41st *Annual Adult Creative Writing Contest* hosted by the Tulsa City-County Library and received an honorable mention in the young adult novel category of the

Oklahoma Writers' Federation Annual Writing Contest. She has been published in the *Tulsa Review, Metaphorosis,* and *Hexagon Speculative Fiction Magazine.* She lives and works in Tulsa, OK.

www.ecfullersbooks.com, @birdshapedhat

Copyright

Title information

Metaphorosis July 2022

ISSN: 2573-136X (online)
ISBN: 978-1-64076-232-9 (e-book)
ISBN: 978-1-64076-233-6 (paperback)

Copyright

Works of fiction

This book contains works of fiction. Characters, dialogue, places, organizations, incidents, and events portrayed in the works are fictional and are products of the author's imagination or used fictitiously. Any resemblance to actual persons, places, organizations, or events is coincidental.

All rights reserved

Moral rights asserted

Each author whose work is included in this book has asserted their moral rights, including the right to be identified as the author of their respective work(s).

Publisher

Metaphorosis
a magazine of speculative fiction

Metaphorosis Magazine is an imprint of
Metaphorosis Publishing
Neskowin, OR, USA

www.metaphorosis.com

"Metaphorosis" is a registered trademark.

Discounts available

Substantial discounts are available for educational institutions, including writing workshops. Discounts are also available for quantity purchases. For details, contact Metaphorosis at metaphorosis.com/about

Metaphorosis Publishing

Metaphorosis offers beautifully written science fiction and fantasy. Our imprints include:

Metaphorosis Magazine
Plant Based Press
Verdage
Vestige

You can also find us:
@MetaphorosisMag, @MetaphorosisRev,
@Metaphorosis
www.facebook.com/metaphorosis

Help keep Metaphorosis running by
supporting us at
Patreon.com/metaphorosis

See more about some of our books on the following pages.

Metaphorosis

a magazine of speculative fiction

Metaphorosis is an online speculative fiction magazine dedicated to quality writing. We publish an original story every week, along with author bios, interviews, and notes on story origins.

We also publish monthly print and e-book issues, as well as yearly Best of and Complete anthologies.

Come and see us online at magazine.Metaphorosis.com.

Metaphorosis
2020
Editor
B. Morris Allen

Metaphorosis
Best of 2019

Metaphorosis
2019
Editor
B. Morris Allen

Metaphorosis
Best of 2018

Metaphorosis
2018
Editor
B. Morris Allen

Metaphorosis
Best of 2017

Metaphorosis
2017
Editor
B. Morris Allen

Metaphorosis
Best of 2016

Metaphorosis
2016
Editor
B. Morris Allen

Plant Based Press

Vegan-friendly science fiction and fantasy, including anthologies of the year's best SFF stories, from 2016-2020.

Chambers of the
Heart

*speculative stories
by
B. Morris Allen*

A heart that's a building, a dog that's a program, a woman sinking irretrievably — stories about love, loss, and movement.

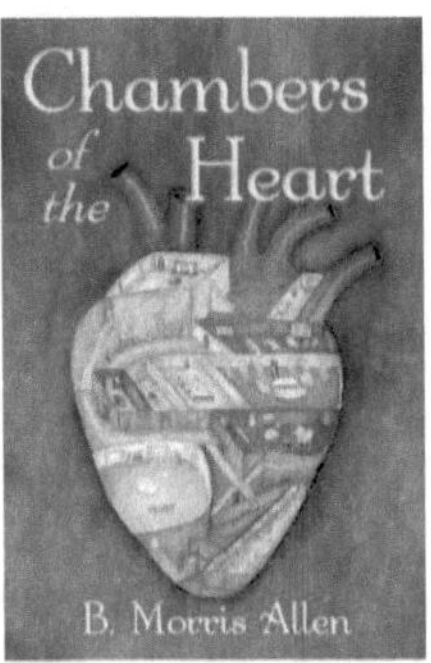

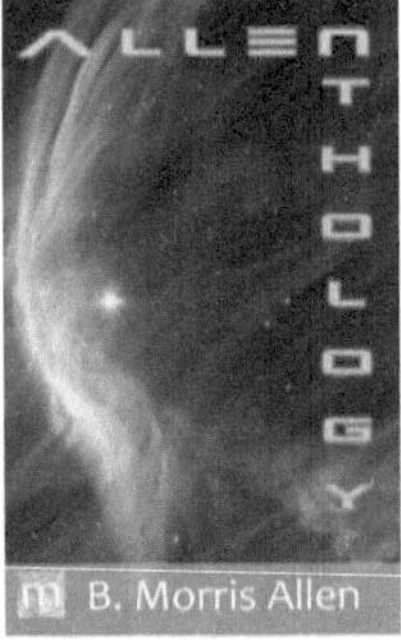

Susurrus

A darkly romantic story of magic, love, and suffering.

Allenthology:
Volume I

Including three full collections of SFF stories.

Verdage

Science fiction and fantasy books for writers – full of great stories, often with an additional focus on the craft of speculative fiction writing.

Reading 5X5 x3

Changes

How do stories move from 'maybe' to published?

Here are 15 case studies of stories published in *Metaphorosis* magazine.

Reading 5X5 x2

Duets

How do authors' voices change when they collaborate?

A round-robin of five talented science fiction and fantasy authors collaborating with each other and writing solo.

Including stories by Evan Marcroft, David Gallay, J. Tynan Burke, L'Erin Ogle, and Douglas Anstruther.

Score

an SFF symphony

An anthology with an emotional score from the heights of joy to the depths of despair – but always with a little hope shining through.

Reading 5X5

Five stories, five times

See how different
writers take on
the same material.

Reading 5X5

Writers' Edition

Two extra stories,
the story seed,
and authors' notes
on writing.

Vestige

Novelettes, novellas, and novels by Metaphorosis authors.

The Nocturnals
Mariah Montoya

Night is Dangerous. Day is deadly.

Where day and night last thirty years, humans move constantly stay ahead of the night and cruel Nocturnals that call it home. But a boy is lost out there.